The Queen Spider

Suddenly Matthew heard a sound. It was like a reel of fishing line unwinding. *Zzzzzzzzzzip!* He spun around to see what it was.

There, dropping down beside Kuros on a long thread of silk, was the biggest spider Matthew had ever seen. The terrifying creature snapped at Kuros, waving her eight arms.

"Run, Kuros!" yelled Matthew. "Run!"

Kuros turned. "I never run from danger," he said. Just then, the spider hit him from behind.

Other Worlds of Power books
you will enjoy:

Blaster Master®
Castlevania II: Simon's Quest®
Metal Gear®
Ninja Gaiden®

WIZARDS & WARRIORS™

A novel based on the best-selling game
by Acclaim™

Book created by F.X. Nine
Written by Ellen Miles
A Seth Godin Production

**This book is not authorized, sponsored, or endorsed
by Nintendo of America Inc.**

SCHOLASTIC INC.
New York Toronto London Auckland Sydney

For my favorite damsels,
Margaret, Sophie, and Katie.

Special thanks to: Greg Holch, Jean Feiwel,
Dick Krinsley, Dona Smith, Eric Leinwand,
Amy Berkower, Sheila Callahan, Nancy Smith,
Joan Giurdanella, and especially Sam Goldberg,
Holly Newman and Allyne Mills.

ISBN 0-590-43769-0

12 11 10 9 8 7 6 5 4 3 2   1 2 3/9

Printed in the U.S.A.   01

First Scholastic printing, September 1990

Chapter One

"And then you just let your imagination *flow,*" said Ms. Underhill. "Enter into that magic land where anything can happen."

Matthew stared out the window. He couldn't *stand* creative writing class. In his opinion, it was easily the worst thing about seventh grade. Ms. Underhill seemed to think that it was the simplest thing in the world to come up with wild ideas and then write stories about them.

And Matthew had to admit that most of the other kids in the class agreed with her. Even his best friend, Michael, had come up with a great idea about skateboarding on Mars. But ideas like that just never seemed to come to Matthew. It was always a struggle trying to think up something new.

He kept looking out the window. Maybe one of those clouds would start to look like something to him, and he could write a story about that. Those clouds...Wow, those clouds were really something. Huge black clouds, looking like they were about to burst. And burst they did. Suddenly it was raining, raining hard. Giant drops splashed against the window and chased each other down the pane.

"Oh, man," muttered Matthew to himself. "Now I won't even get to try out Michael's new ramp." Michael's dad had finally agreed to help him build a ramp for skateboarding, and Matthew was dying to check it out. Think of the moves they'd be able to get down with such a great place to practice. But now it was pouring. "Oh, man," said Matthew again, sighing loudly.

"Mr. Lukens?" said Ms. Underhill. "Do you have something to contribute?" Matthew looked up, startled. What was he supposed to say?

"Uh, no...I guess not," he said. A few of the girls giggled, and Matthew felt himself blushing. The bell rang, and he bolted out of his seat. School hadn't ended a moment too soon.

The house was empty and quiet when Matthew got home, but he was used to that. His parents both worked pretty late, most days. And most days, Matthew would be out skateboarding until dark. But today he was stuck inside. What a drag.

He walked through the house, turning on

lights as he went. No reason to hang around in a gloomy room. The kitchen was kind of a mess — everyone had been in a hurry that morning. The sink was full of breakfast dishes, and a dirty frying pan sat on the stove. Working around the mess, Matthew made himself a snack. Maybe he'd clean up later, if he didn't find anything better to do.

He sat at the table, reading the sports page and munching on his peanut butter and sardine sandwich. The sports page was boring. His sandwich was boring. Face it, thought Matthew. This is a boring afternoon.

He put his plate into the sink, along with the other dishes, and walked out of the kitchen. He wandered into his father's study. Maybe there'd be something interesting to look at in there. No such luck. His dad's desk was basically empty — you know those lawyers, always so organized — and the shelves along the wall were filled with dull stuff like law books and family pictures.

Matthew stepped closer to look at an old picture of himself in a cowboy outfit. Then he saw the knight.

The knight stood behind a picture frame, carelessly hidden away. Its armor was dusty, and an old cobweb hung from one arm. The figure was only a couple of inches high, but dusty as it was it seemed to stand proudly.

Matthew remembered that knight. He remembered how many times he'd begged his dad to let him play with it. "Maybe when you're older," his dad would say. "When you're old enough, but not *too* old. That's when we'll take him down." Old enough but not too old, thought Matthew. I'd have to say that describes me right now. Anyway, what's the big deal about a toy knight?

He picked up the figure and headed out of the room. The toy felt heavy in his hand. Matthew took the stairs two at a time and pushed open the door to his bedroom. What a mess. Matthew's mom called his decorating scheme "Early American Dirty Sock." But Matthew felt comfortable in his room, and he knew just where everything was.

Now, where were those jams? Matthew was ready to change out of his school clothes, and even though he wasn't going to be doing any skateboarding, he felt like wearing his favorite jams. He'd gotten them for his last birthday, and he had to admit his mom had pretty good taste. They had pink, black, and yellow checkerboards on them. Matthew brushed off his night table, knocking some rock-hard orange peels to the floor, and set the knight down gently.

He rummaged through the top drawer in his dresser, looking for the jams. Where could they be? Suddenly he froze. What was that clanking sound? He stopped to listen, and the sound stopped, too. It was probably just the fridge defrosting itself. Matthew turned to his closet and dug into the pile of dirty clothes that lay on the floor. Maybe he'd thrown the jams in there, even though he'd only worn them six or seven times this week. They were hardly what you could call dirty.

"Aha!" There they were. Matthew took off his school pants and pulled on the jams. He was facing the closet, and his back was to the rest of the room, but suddenly he had the distinct feeling that there was someone in there with him.

"Kaajjhooo!" A loud sneeze broke the silence. Matthew whirled around. He saw his bed, unmade as usual. He saw his desk, piled high with junk. He saw the blue-and-beige rag rug on the floor next to his bed, and standing on the rug, he saw ...

A knight. A hulking giant of a man, wearing body armor with finely tooled metal bands around his massive arms. A scabbard set with jewels hung at his side. The man shook back his long, thick hair to expose a face that was noble and kind. "Forgive me, Squire," he said. "The dust, methinks." The knight rubbed his nose, grinning shyly.

Chapter Two

Matthew's jaw dropped. This couldn't be happening. Knights just don't appear in suburban bedrooms. What was going on? He rubbed his eyes. Obviously, he was seeing things. Must have been those sardines — he'd have to go easier on them next time.

He turned back to the closet, looking for a shirt to change into, and then slowly turned around to make sure that the apparition had disappeared. It hadn't. The knight still stood there, adjusting his armor.

"Okay. Who are you, and what do you want? Is this some kind of a joke? One of those singing telegrams or something?" Matthew asked. No phony knight was going to make *him* look like a chump.

"Singing? I am not singing," said the knight. "They call me Kuros, Squire. I am a knight of the Enchanted Realms. On this day

I begin the most important journey of my life. A quest."

Matthew waited, with raised eyebrows. He wasn't convinced.

"I've come to ask you to accompany me, as my squire," continued the knight. "I go to the land of Elrond. I have been alone for many years, and company would soothe my heart and ease my journey. Wilt thou come?"

"Wait a minute," said Matthew. "You want me to come with you on this trip, this quest? How do I know it'll be safe? I mean, I can't afford to get hurt or anything."

"It *won't* be safe," said Kuros. "It will be fraught with unimaginable dangers and terrors — but only for me. You should be safe, as you are of another world. The demons I battle will never see you or hear you, even though you may be by my side."

"Huh," said Matthew. "I could live with that, I guess. So what's the story with this quest thing? What's it all about?"

"Sit down, Squire," said Kuros. "This might take a while."

Matthew sat on the end of his bed, and Kuros made himself comfortable on the rug.

"You've no doubt heard of the Wizard Malkil, most evil of them all?" Matthew shook his head. Kuros raised his eyebrows, but continued. "Malkil was once one of the greatest wizards of time remembered. He taught the most venerable and honored Merlin, of whom you *must* have heard." Matthew nodded.

"But while Merlin worked only good enchantments, Malkil has gone over to the dark side. He is very, very old and has experimented with too many potions. He has become bitter, insane, and evil."

Matthew was getting restless. This *was* going to be a long story, unless he could get Kuros to move along. "So what does all of this have to do with the quest?" he asked. This was really too weird. He couldn't believe he was sitting here in his own bedroom, listening to a knight tell stories.

Kuros looked sad. "Malkil has captured the beautiful and clever Princess Miranda. He has taken her away, along with six of her most trusted handmaidens. He has hidden the handmaidens all over Elrond, and he has taken the princess to his Castle IronSpire. We must rescue the princess and all of the other damsels, and put an end to Malkil. And we must do it before the sun sets on this day."

"Rescue damsels, kill a wizard. That doesn't sound all that tough," said Matthew. "You should have no problem taking care of the wizard with that wicked-looking machete you've got." Matthew pointed at the scabbard that hung at Kuros's side.

"Machete? This is no machete!" thundered Kuros. "This is BrightSword, known far and wide as the most noble weapon of them all. I had the magical BrightSword made to fit my hand perfectly by the Elves of Applemear.

BrightSword has vanquished uncountable evildoers and is still as sharp as the day it was forged." Kuros began to calm down. "What *is* a machete, anyway?" he asked sheepishly.

Matthew shook his head. "It isn't important. Go on."

Kuros continued. "Even with BrightSword, the quest will be full of dangers. Elrond has become an evil land, full of traps set by Malkil. And the Castle IronSpire is an enchanted place. Even the bravest knights have failed to reach its inner keep. But together you and I will succeed. We will have BrightSword, and I have learned of many other amulets, charmed weaponry, and talismans that will aid us in our quest. Remember, too, that the power of good is with us. Even Malkil must shrink before such force."

"Sounds okay," said Matthew. "But you didn't explain why we have to complete the quest by sundown. What's the deal with that?"

"Malkil has threatened that at sundown tonight he will put an end to Princess Miranda. He says he grows tired of holding her prisoner. He also threatens to destroy the entire land of Elrond, permanently," said Kuros. "And Malkil's threats are not often empty."

Matthew thought for a minute. Kuros didn't seem to think they'd have any trouble completing the quest by sundown. What did he have to lose? Kuros said that he'd be safe . . . and it sounded like it might be fun. He couldn't go skateboarding anyway, and what else was he going to do? Maybe the whole thing would give him some great new ideas for creative writing. Even Michael had never thought of writing about a knightly quest.

He closed his eyes for a minute. Was he really going to do this? Take off into an enchanted land with a knight who'd turned up in his bedroom? He shrugged. "Okay, I'm set. Let's go!" he said. "How do we get there?"

Kuros didn't answer. He just got up, checked on his sword and scabbard, and strode to the bedroom door. He grabbed the doorknob, turned it, and flung the door open, all in one motion. Matthew, now standing on the rag rug where Kuros had been, looked up and felt his knees turn to water.

> ## GAME HINT
>
> Don't fight the bees inside the hollow bee tree. Keep moving down until you find the Wand of Wonder.

Chapter Three

Instead of orange shag carpeting, Matthew saw, outside his bedroom door, a covering of dirt and leaves. And instead of a hallway leading to the bathroom, he saw...a forest.

The forest of Elrond was a quiet place. Not quiet *peaceful*, Matthew decided, but quiet in an uncomfortable way. As if the whole forest were just waiting for something—anything—to happen.

It was dark, too, even though it wasn't night—Matthew could see tiny rays of sunshine doing their best to reach through the heavy canopy above. The overlapping branches of the trees were hung with vines, and vines also crept down tree trunks and across the forest floor.

Birds flitted between the trees—if birds as big as these could be said to flit. They looked about the size of Thanksgiving turkeys, to Matthew. None of the birds was singing.

Matthew did not have a good feeling about this forest, and he turned to Kuros to say so. But Kuros wasn't beside him. Matthew whirled around, his heart beating wildly.

Being in the forest was bad enough, but if he were here alone, without Kuros, without BrightSword . . . Oh, man. But Kuros wasn't in sight. "Kuros," Matthew called. His voice sounded weak and puny in the huge silence of the forest. He cleared his throat. "Kuros!" he called, louder this time. There was no answer.

Matthew started to walk down what looked like a path, but then he stopped. He had no idea where he was, or worse yet, where he might end up if he followed some path. He looked around for a comfortable spot to sit, thinking that he might just as well stay in one spot until Kuros showed up.

Just then, he heard something. It wasn't bird song, and it wasn't a squirrel or any other creature you might expect to hear in a forest.

Whooosh! Whooosh! Whup-whup-whup-whup! Even though it was a sound unlike any that Matthew had ever heard before, somehow he knew just what it was. It was BrightSword!

Matthew ran toward the sound, leaping over huge roots and dodging dangling vines.

He entered a small clearing and saw Kuros. The knight was surrounded by a swarm of hornets — deadly looking hornets, the size of small birds.

Kuros's face was calm, but his body was in frantic motion. BrightSword flashed as the knight slashed and jabbed at the terrifying horde of enemies. Hornets lay in piles around the clearing, but more continued to appear as Kuros fought on.

Matthew drew as close as he dared. The hornets ignored his presence completely. He felt totally useless — if only there were some way he could help. But Kuros seemed to have the situation under control. He was breathing hard, and his brow glistened with sweat, but now that Matthew was closer he could see that Kuros was, amazingly, smiling. This must be the kind of thing that knights *live* for, Matthew realized.

Finally Kuros fought his way out of the swarm. He had reduced its numbers by at least half, and the remaining insects flew off in a hurry. Kuros looked exhausted. He wasn't smiling anymore as he staggered toward the tree that Matthew was leaning against.

"All *right!*" said Matthew, holding up his hand for a high five. Kuros looked at him quizzically. He held up his own hand and stood there looking like a traffic cop.

"Yes, I am all right," he said. "But though BrightSword is the finest weapon I have ever carried, I must confess that it is not made for this kind of combat. It is too heavy for such fighting. I cannot swing a weapon of this weight forever." He paused. "Why do we hold our hands up like this, Squire?"

Matthew laughed. "I'm waiting for you to pop me a high five," he said. "Like this." He smacked Kuros's hand with his own. It means . . . it means that I congratulate you for doing well."

"I thank you, Squire, though this battle was mere child's play compared with what we must face ahead. Still, I would like to rest for just a moment." Kuros tottered to another tree and leaned against it, then slid to a sitting position. His head sagged against the tree, and Matthew saw something amazing.

A small door had opened in the tree's trunk. It must have been a magic door — it appeared out of nowhere, and Matthew couldn't see any hinges or hardware attached to it. Kuros must have hit some kind of button as he slid to the ground. Matthew saw a scrap of bright red just inside the opening. What could it be?

Matthew reached in, gingerly. What if those hornets had a nest around here somewhere? He groped around and pulled out an odd package. The wrapping was a length of beautiful, soft red leather.

Matthew sat down next to Kuros and held the package on his lap.

Matthew wasn't sure if he should open

the package, but it was impossible to resist peeking. He lifted one end of the leather and looked inside. A bright red stone caught a tiny ray of sunshine and flashed it into Matthew's eyes. "Wow!" said Matthew, out loud.

Kuros sat up with a snort. "What! What! Are we being attacked?" He looked around wildly and saw Matthew next to him, holding the package on his lap. "What have we here, Squire?" he asked.

Matthew handed the package to the knight. "You open it," he said. Kuros pulled at the leather, and it fell open to reveal a small dagger, forged of gold and set with gleaming jewels. Matthew gasped. Kuros smiled broadly.

"Matthew, my squire. You have found the weapon I need most right now. This is the Dagger of Throwing! Canst thou believe it?" He held up his hand, grinning. Matthew smiled back and smacked the knight's palm. This guy caught on fast.

"This dagger will be a great boon in our quest," said Kuros. He stood and stretched. "Let us continue. We must hunt for the gems that will ease our passage through this land. I have been told that Malkil hides these gems in the treetops. If we can find some way to reach them, we will be rich indeed."

Matthew hadn't climbed a tree for years, but he remembered when he'd been the tree-climbing champ of the whole neighborhood. He looked around for a likely candidate.

When he found one with good low branches that would hold him, he started up it. It didn't take long before he was high above the ground. "Hellooo, down there," he called. Kuros was looking up at him anxiously.

"Do you see a small chest up there, my squire?" the knight called. Matthew parted the branches and glanced around. Sure enough, there was a little brown chest perched in the crook of a branch, almost hidden by leaves. He reached for it and climbed back down clumsily, carrying the chest. When he hit the ground, Kuros took it from him eagerly and opened it. It was full of gleaming gems: Rubies, emeralds, diamonds, and pearls shone in the weak sunlight.

Kuros grinned and scooped up a handful. He stuffed them into his pockets. Matthew followed his lead and did the same, and soon the chest was empty. "Now, teach me how to ascend the trees," said the knight.

Soon Kuros was climbing as high as Matthew. He was clumsy in his armor, but he was so determined to get up the trees that nothing could stop him. In one tree, a vicious swarm of flies attacked the knight, but he fought them off gleefully with his new weapon. The dagger shone as it flew through the air, taking on a life of its own and flashing through the swarm until every last fly disappeared.

Before long, their pockets were bulging with jewels so that they could hardly walk,

16

much less climb more trees. They moved slowly through the forest. "Malkil must sense our presence," said Kuros. "He knows that we are coming. He sends his 'helpers' to try to slow us down."

"And here come more now," yelled Matthew, as a cloud of bats swooped out of the sky in perfect formation. They flew at Kuros, diving at his face. They seemed to be trying to herd him away from a certain tree, Matthew noticed. He decided to take advantage of the fact that the bats didn't seem to see him.

As Kuros fought mightily, throwing the dagger again and again, Matthew slipped around to the tree and inspected it. Looking closely, he saw a small gray door. There was a tiny keyhole and a little doorknob set above it.

Did he need a key to open this door? Matthew looked over at Kuros, who was just fighting off the last of the bats. With one last perfectly aimed throw, the knight ended another small battle. He walked to Matthew's side, looked at the door, and tried the knob. The door swung open, and Matthew saw that it led into the tree. By hunching over and making themselves as small as possible, Kuros and Matthew were able to get through the door.

Inside, the tree was much larger than it had looked. It was like being in a small room. And glinting in the darkness was a gleaming chest of gold. Matthew walked over to it and touched it cautiously. The chest opened. What a snap, thought Matthew. This quest stuff isn't so hard.

Kuros peered over Matthew's shoulder at the gorgeous boots that lay in the chest. "Squire, you have done it again. First you find the Dagger of Throwing, and now you discover the legendary Boots of Force. Do you realize what this means?" asked the delighted knight.

"Uh ... no, I guess not," said Matthew. Was this some kind of ? How was he supposed to know?

"A good hard kick from these boots will open almost any chest in the kingdom of Elrond," said the knight. "Malkil can put his strongest spells on their locks, but these boots are stronger yet. Look at them! Are they not beautiful?"

"Well, they're not exactly my style," said Matthew. But I'm sure they'll come in handy."

Kuros sat down and pulled off his own boots and threw them aside. He pulled one of the boots out of the chest and drew it on. "Look at the workmanship," he said. "This is the finest leather I have ever seen." He pulled on the other. The cuffed tops of both were encrusted with shining jewels. He stood and looked down admiringly.

"Let's go," said Matthew. The boots *were* pretty incredible, but after all, they were only boots. Kuros followed Matthew back out of the tree and the two continued down the path they were following.

As they walked, Matthew began explaining the concept of a Walkman to Kuros, who had never even heard of a radio. It was clear to Matthew that the knight had a lot to learn about the world. "See, it has these little headphones, and you can put in a tape — " he was saying. Kuros nodded wisely, not understanding a word.

Suddenly, both of them stopped in their tracks. Ahead stood another human, the first they'd seen in the forest. It was a knight, dressed all in red from head to toe. His shield was red. His scabbard was red. His boots were red. Matthew turned white and stopped talking. Kuros drew BrightSword. The Red Knight yawned.

GAME HINT

When you find a turkey drumstick, grab it. It will give you extra life.

Chapter Four

The Red Knight stood there, blocking the way. "What do we do now, Kuros?" asked Matthew.

"I'll handle this," said the knight. He turned to the Red Knight and spoke loudly. "I am Kuros, Knight of the Enchanted Realms. My squire, Matthew, accompanies me. Let us pass."

"No." The Red Knight said only that one word, but he said it with force.

Kuros held BrightSword up. "Shall we fight for our right to pass?" he asked, advancing toward the Red Knight. But the man in red did not draw his sword. He just stood there.

"You do not wish to make swordplay with me? I don't blame you. The names of Kuros and BrightSword are known far and wide," said Kuros. The Red Knight did not even flinch at the insult. He just stood there.

"Shall we fight with staves?" asked Kuros. "Matthew, fetch me a staff. Cut one of those saplings, there." Matthew looked around. He didn't know the first thing about making a staff. Some squire he was. But it didn't matter, because the Red Knight didn't have a staff either, and he didn't start to look for one. He just stood there.

"What is it you want, then?" asked Kuros finally. "We want to pass, yet you will not allow it. Neither will you fight. How shall this end?"

"Gems." Again, the Red Knight spoke firmly.

"Oh-ho! I see how it is now. You want a toll," Kuros said, smiling. "Well, if it's gems you want, it's gems you shall have." He reached into his pocket and pulled out a handful of rubies. He handed them to the Red Knight. The man's hand closed around them, but then he spoke again.

"More."

"More?" asked Kuros. He shrugged and reached into another pocket. He pulled out a handful of emeralds and handed them over. But it still wasn't enough. The Red Knight was not satisfied. Kuros cleaned out his pockets down to the last pearl and the Red Knight was still not satisfied. "How many do you want?" asked Kuros finally.

"One hundred." The knight was firm. It was obvious that he would not bargain with them. Kuros had already given him thirty-five gems, and now it was Matthew's turn to empty out his pockets. He parted reluctantly with every diamond he had, but they were still short of the toll the Red Knight demanded.

There was nothing to do but to go back and find more gems. And Matthew knew they'd better move quickly. The sun was already high in the sky, and the day would not last forever.

They were both tired of climbing trees by now, so Matthew was happy to spot a chest half hidden in the undergrowth. "Kuros, come quick. I'll bet the gems we need will be in this chest," he called. Together they tried to open the chest, but the locks held tight.

"Never fear, Squire," said Kuros. "I shall use the Boots of Force."

He kicked gently at the chest. It didn't open. He kicked harder. The chest stayed shut tight. "Accursed things," cried Kuros, frowning at the boots. He was about to tear them off, when Matthew noticed a ruby on one of the cuffs. It was glowing like a Christmas-tree light.

Matthew touched the ruby. The boots seemed to glow all over for a moment, and he thought he heard a hum. "Try again," he said.

Kuros kicked the chest, and the lid flew up to reveal a huge pile of gleaming gems. "We're saved!" he said.

"Guess those boots just needed to be turned on," said Matthew, as they headed back to pay off the Red Knight.

After the Red Knight had accepted the exact toll without speaking, Matthew and Kuros continued on their way. They were getting to know the forest now: Matthew could almost predict when a swarm of bats would attack, and he knew enough to warn Kuros when he saw the giant spiders dropping down out of the trees.

Kuros had a good eye for finding the well hidden small bottles of magic potions that helped him to fight off their enemies. Malkil must have hidden the potions for his own use, but Kuros helped himself. He said he'd studied up on the potions he might find on his quest, and that he knew which ones to try.

Matthew thought the knight was crazy the first time he saw him drink down a nasty-looking pink potion — but he had to admit that he'd never seen Kuros jump higher than right after he had drunk it. Still, Matthew wouldn't touch any of the potions when Kuros offered them. Who knew what was in them? The red one seemed especially strong — it seemed to make Kuros completely invincible, if only for a few seconds.

Kuros had just downed a blue potion, which helped him to move incredibly fast, when they were attacked by hornets again. Between the potion and the Dagger of

Throwing, Kuros made light work of them. He'd learned a lot since he had first entered the forest.

Not long after, Matthew was walking alone, looking for gems, when he stumbled over a bright red chest. "Kuros, the boots!" he called. But when Kuros looked at the chest, he told Matthew that the boots would not work on a chest colored like this.

"We'll need to find a key for this one," said Kuros. "But it may be worth our while. The key will most probably be somewhere nearby."

Matthew and the knight scoured the area, turning over rocks and brushing away leaves. Suddenly Matthew saw something glinting in between two rocks.

"Is this it?" Matthew asked, holding up a red key. A vine hung over his shoulder and his hair was full of leaves. His face was smudged with dirt. But Kuros looked at him as if he were the greatest thing he'd ever seen.

"Yes, my squire, that is it," said Kuros. They tried the key in the chest, and sure enough the lid creaked open. Inside, Matthew saw what looked like the trunk lid of his dad's car, all rusty and stained.

But Kuros was overcome with emotion. "By the Round Table! This is none other than the Shield of Protection! " He pulled it out. "Help me put it on, Squire. I'll need this to get past Malkil's evil guardians."

Matthew privately thought that Kuros looked kind of ratty with the shield on, but he held his tongue as they continued on through the forest. After all, Kuros was doing all the fighting. They'd never have made it this far if he hadn't been the warrior that he was. If he said the shield was a good idea, Matthew wasn't going to argue.

Chapter Five

The path they were following wound through the trees, but never seemed to bring them any closer to the edge of the forest. The undergrowth was still just as thick as when they had begun their journey, and the sun had not gotten any stronger. Matthew was tired of the forest, and he could see that Kuros was becoming exhausted from fighting off every evil creature that came their way. "Let's rest for a moment," he said.

They found a tiny spot of sun, and settled down with their backs against a log. "I could sure use a Coke right now," said Matthew. "And some Doritos would be great." Kuros didn't answer. He was asleep. Matthew closed his eyes, too. A nap couldn't hurt.

"*Cuckoo! Cuckoo!*" What was *that?* Matthew woke with a start. Kuros had been woken also. They looked at each other. "*Cuckoo!*" There it was again. It sounded as if it came from behind the log they leaned against. Matthew reached back and pulled out a cuckoo clock.

"Boy, you don't see this kind of clock too often," said Matthew. All of the clocks in his house were digital. Kuros was fascinated by the timepiece, and together they figured out how it worked.

"Have you noticed something, my squire?" asked Kuros. "When the clock goes off, it seems that every motion in the forest freezes. Methinks this may be an enchanted clock!"

"This may be our ticket out of the forest!" said Matthew. "Let's carry it with us." They got up and stretched, then continued on their path. Without warning, a swarm of flying ants enveloped them.

Kuros drew the dagger, but Matthew told him to wait. He activated the clock. *Cuckoo! Cuckoo!* The ants froze in place, and Matthew and Kuros walked away with no trouble. "Awesome!" said Matthew.

"Yes, I, too, am full of awe," said Kuros. He sheathed his dagger and led the way. They walked on, using the clock occasionally to freeze Malkil's "helpers," until they began to come close to the edge of the forest.

Matthew's heart rose at the sight of the sun, up ahead through the trees. Finally! But then he saw the eagles. Five or six of them, circling silently. "Malkil's flying soldiers," said Kuros under his breath. "Beware."

Matthew had never thought that eagles would be frightening, but these birds were *big*. And mean-looking. They seemed to be watching something below them, and as Matthew drew closer he saw what it was.

It was a girl — the most beautiful girl he'd ever seen. Even more beautiful than Karin Douglas, who sat in the row next to him in algebra. This girl was wearing a long green gown — the exact green of the forest's trees.

She was tied securely to one of those trees — the biggest one Matthew had seen yet. The eagles were guarding her, it was plain to see. Without much hope, Matthew tried the clock. *"Cuckoo! Cuckoo!"* But the eagles kept circling. And then they started to dive.

Kuros drew both the dagger and Bright-Sword and set to work. Matthew turned to the girl. He realized that this must be one of the "damsels" he'd heard about — one of Princess Miranda's handmaidens. He'd never met a damsel before. What was he supposed to call her? Your damselness?

"What's your name?" she asked. "I'm Lucinda. Can you untie me?"

She sounded so normal! "Sure!" Matthew said.

"Sure?" she asked. "That is your name — Sure?"

Matthew blushed. "No, no. I meant sure, I'd untie you. My name's Matthew. Matthew

Lukens. And that's Kuros. He's my squire. I mean, I'm *his* squire. He's a knight. But you can see that, by the way he's fighting off those eagles." Matthew felt like a jerk. He was babbling, just like he always did in front of a pretty girl. He set to work and untied the ropes that held Lucinda.

He finished just as Kuros finished off the last of the eagles. Kuros joined Matthew and Lucinda.

"I don't know how to thank you," said Lucinda. " I thought my life was over. Malkil's eagles make excellent jailers."

"So you *are* one of the damsels," said Matthew. "Great! Now we're really on the right track. We're on our way to the Castle IronSpire to rescue the Princess Miranda." He felt a lot more confident with Kuros towering by his side.

But what were they supposed to do with Lucinda, drag her along with them? She looked like a strong, healthy girl, but how much could she really help them, all dressed up in that gown?

Before he could wonder any farther, Lucinda thanked them again, gave them a few hints about the path ahead, and walked off. She'd only gone about ten steps when Matthew saw her gown turn to pure white. Then she disappeared. He rubbed his eyes and looked again, but she was definitely gone. The most beautiful girl he'd ever seen, and she'd disappeared into thin air. Just his luck.

Chapter Six

As suddenly as they had entered the forest, Matthew and Kuros left it. One moment they were walking beneath entangled vines, and the next there was nothing above them but the sun. And the sun felt delicious.

Matthew breathed deeply, as if he were trying to clear the musty smell of dead leaves and moss from his nose. He looked up, enjoying the sight of blue sky instead of the endless green he'd been looking at for so long. He looked over at Kuros and smiled. The knight was also clearly happy to be out of the forest. His noble face was turned to the sun, and his now-battered armor glinted in its rays.

No bats flew near them; no spiders dropped down. It was a relief to be away from Malkil's "helpers."

The landscape in front of them was strange, thought Matthew, kind of empty and flat, dotted with huge boulders. It didn't look like any place Matthew had ever been before.

He and Kuros began to walk toward one of the most gigantic boulders.

"Let us sit for a moment while we plan our next move," said Kuros.

Matthew agreed. The sun felt nice and warm on his shoulders — he wouldn't mind sitting and soaking it up for a few minutes. When he and Kuros arrived at the rock, they both flopped down next to it. The rock radiated warmth from the sun, and Matthew leaned against it. The rock moved aside as if it were made of Styrofoam.

Matthew and Kuros were falling before they knew what had happened. Down, down, down, they slid, into a sloping tunnel that had been hidden by the rock. Matthew couldn't even tell which way was up anymore, not in the pitch-black darkness that surrounded him. He heard the clanking of Kuros's armor, and the gasps the knight made as he tried to stop his fall. Well, at least they were together.

Matthew tried to catch onto the walls of the tunnel, but they were as slick as glass. Finally he gave up and just let himself slide.

It seemed as if they'd been falling for hours, although Matthew knew it had probably only been seconds. Suddenly Matthew heard a thud as Kuros hit bottom. Almost immediately, Matthew fell hard too, right on top of Kuros. *"Oof!"* said the knight.

They disentangled themselves, stood up, and brushed each other off. Then they looked around. Blue. Matthew saw nothing but blue wherever he looked. They were in some kind of a cave, and the walls of the cave gave off an eerie blue glow. The floor of the cave was also blue, and the ceiling was covered in huge blue stalactites. "Nice decorating scheme," Matthew said aloud.

Kuros looked grim. "I feel Malkil's presence here," he said. "His evil lurks in the very walls of this cave." As Kuros spoke, Matthew felt a chill run over his body.

"Let's get going," said Matthew. "This place gives me the creeps. Which way is out?"

Kuros looked around and nodded at a cave branching off to the right. "Let's try this one," he said. The knight led the way, hand on his sword. Matthew followed, glancing back over his shoulder occasionally. The caves were quiet, but somehow Matthew did not feel as if he and Kuros were entirely alone.

They followed the cave they had entered for a while, and then came upon a fork. They took another right, and yet another at the next fork. After that they took three lefts, another right, and then two more lefts. The caves seemed never-ending, and the blue walls just seemed to glow more and more blue as they got deeper into the caves.

Matthew trudged along behind Kuros, his head hanging. He felt exhausted, as if he could fall asleep while he walked. Suddenly his head jerked up. A loud chattering noise rang in his ears as a horde of ghostlike creatures surrounded him.

The creatures shimmered in the dim blue light, darting toward Kuros and then quickly away, before he could lunge at them with BrightSword. Matthew reached out to grab onto Kuros, and felt his hand pass through one of the horrible phantoms. *"Ugh!"* he cried, shaking his hand as though he could rid it of the cold, slimy feeling. "Kuros!" he said. "The Dagger of Throwing!"

The knight reached for the small dagger, aimed quickly, and threw. It whipped through the air, flashing as it cut through the spooks. Matthew heard unearthly shrieks as the apparitions flickered and disappeared. The blue air was full of their howls. Kuros fought on. Matthew's ears were being tortured by the terrifying sounds, and he was tempted to cover them, but he could see that Kuros needed his help.

The knight could not keep all the ghosts in view. They appeared and disappeared as they attacked. Matthew kept track as best he could, yelling to warn Kuros as each spook reappeared. Finally the last shriek echoed through the cave. Kuros dropped to his knees, exhausted. "Kuros!" yelled Matthew. "Watch out!"

One last ghost had swept down from above, and was on top of the knight almost before he could react. It was too late to throw the dagger, but Kuros struggled to plunge it into the creature that was nearly suffocating him. Another shriek, and then all was quiet.

Matthew let out his breath. Kuros sat with his eyes closed, leaning against the wall of the cave. Matthew looked closer. Kuros was smiling.

"I don't believe it," said Matthew.

Kuros opened one eye. "What it is that you do not believe, my squire?" he asked.

"First we fight our way through the whole length of that nasty forest. Then we finally get out, but can we enjoy being in the sun? No!" said Matthew. "As soon as we have one minute to relax, we fall down into some huge pit and end up in these blue caves. We're probably totally lost and someday somebody will find our bones here. Meanwhile, we get attacked by a squad of ghosts, we nearly get killed, and only by luck do you manage to destroy the last one! And yet you sit there smiling. I don't believe it."

"First of all, Squire, it was not luck," said Kuros, still smiling. "It was your timely warning that allowed me to vanquish my final enemy. You are the finest squire I have ever had."

Matthew blushed and shoved his hands into his pockets. "Yeah, well . . ."

"And I am smiling for a good reason," continued Kuros. "Sit down. Let me tell you a story."

Chapter Seven

Matthew made himself comfortable on the blue floor of the cave.

"I grew up in Elrond," began Kuros. "And I was not always a knight. I come from humble beginnings. My father was a miller. Folk came from miles around, bringing their corn and wheat to be milled with his stones. They knew his mill was as good as the king's, and they knew him for the fair man that he was."

"Was?" asked Matthew. He looked closer at the knight. Kuros wasn't smiling anymore. His eyes had darkened, and his face was full of a deep sadness.

Kuros nodded. "And my mother," he went on. "She was a weaver, one of the best in the land. She could take the wool of our sheep and turn it into shawls and tunics of the most incredible warmth and beauty." He paused for a moment.

Matthew cleared his throat, and the

knight looked up. "My mother, yes. She was a beauty, herself. I have heard tales of how, in her youth, she was the envy of every damsel in Elrond. She was also the desire of every fellow. But my father won her heart with his goodness and kind ways." Kuros turned his head, but it was too late. Matthew had already seen it — a single tear, glistening in the corner of the knight's eye.

"Kuros," said Matthew gently. "I'm so sorry. How did they die?"

"Die?" asked Kuros. "They are not dead, but perhaps they would be better off if they were." He brushed away the tear and looked straight at Matthew. "Elrond was once a happy land, full of life and love. That was before Malkil. When I was ten-and-seven, Malkil made his presence known in Elrond. Town by town, village by village, he terrorized the people and made them pay him homage. And then that was not enough. He was bored. Then he enchanted them, froze them in time." Kuros's mouth was a grim, straight line. "They are not dead, but they know not life."

Matthew shuddered. He felt as if Malkil was in the cave with them, breathing his cold breath over his shoulder. This guy was powerful! This was no game Matthew was involved in, no comic-book quest. This was for real! Malkil had to be stopped.

"But I still don't get it, " he said. "Why do you smile as you fight? You almost look happy."

"This is why, my squire," said Kuros. "Listen. When Malkil enchanted my people, he took their souls and left them as empty husks. Then he did his evil magic with each soul, and formed the evil creatures that you have seen me fighting."

Matthew nodded. "So what happens when the Dagger of Throwing cuts through one of them?" he asked.

Kuros smiled. "Each time I slay one of Malkil's creations, an honest citizen of Elrond is restored to life. That is why I smile. I like to imagine my dear friends walking and talking again, their souls returned to them none the worse for wear."

Matthew smiled back. "That's great! No wonder you look so happy while you fight," he said. "And I'm sure you'll see your parents again someday soon." His smile faded. "If we can find our way out of these caves, that is." Matthew thought of his own parents. They seemed so far away. Would he ever see them again? Was there any way out of Elrond, even if he did find his way out of this blue maze?

"Worry not, my squire," said Kuros. The knight's large hand rested on Matthew's shoulder. "We will take one step at at time, and fate will not betray us." Kuros struggled to his feet, and held out a hand to Matthew. Matthew grabbed it and stood. They looked at each other and smiled.

"Let's go!" said Kuros, holding up his hand.

Matthew grinned. He raised his own hand and slapped the knight's, then fell into step behind him.

Matthew felt more cheerful now. He felt a sense of purpose. But a sense of purpose didn't help much with his fear that they were lost in a maze of blue caves. You couldn't even call it a fear anymore, he thought. It was a fact. They were lost.

They had taken countless right forks and almost an equal number of lefts. Every cave looked exactly like the one before. There were no landmarks, no guideposts, no way to know that they weren't just going in circles.

Kuros led on. He seemed confident, but Matthew was beginning to wonder. How could Kuros have any idea where they were or where they were going?

Suddenly Kuros stopped, and Matthew bumped up against him. When he stepped back, he saw why the knight had halted. There was a wall in front of them. A blue wall, of course. There were no forks here to the right *or* to the left. They had come to a dead end.

"We'll have to turn back and retrace our steps," said Kuros.

Matthew nodded wearily. It was the only option, but what good would it do? They'd never find their way back to the original tunnel they'd fallen down, and even if they could, so what? They'd never be able to climb back out. Malkil had entrapped them like rats in his evil blue maze.

He turned to go back, but saw only another blue wall in front of him. Wait a minute! Hadn't there just been a tunnel there? Matthew spun around wildly. His heart was palpitating and his breath came in gasps. There was no tunnel. There was no way out! He and Kuros were trapped in a small room, a room with curving blue walls. And the room seemed to be growing smaller every second.

Chapter Eight

The room had shrunk to the size of Matthew's bedroom. Then it got even smaller, until it was like being shut in the hall closet. Except it was blue. Matthew suddenly hated the color blue, which until now had been his favorite. He felt like he was suffocating in blue, drowning in blue. He couldn't breathe.

But Kuros looked calm, as always. "This must be Malkil's work," he said. "We can't let him stop us now."

"But what can we do?" asked Matthew, gasping for air. The room seemed even smaller now, if that was possible. He and Kuros were squeezed shoulder to shoulder. "Your weapons are no use against this!"

Kuros nodded. "That is right, Squire. But we have other weapons, the only weapons that will work against such evil. We have the weapons of truth and good."

"Right." Matthew felt deflated. What

good were truth and good going to do in a situation like this? Maybe Kuros was just stalling while he tried to think of a *real* solution. Matthew groped along the walls blindly, looking for a crack or an opening. His hands felt a small ledge, and there was something on the ledge. He grabbed the small item and looked at it. A red key. Big help that was, right now. He put it in his pocket.

"Quickly, Squire," said Kuros. "Tell me a truth. Tell it to the walls. Tell it to the world. Tell a truth you have not told before."

Matthew looked at Kuros. Had the knight gone crazy? Kuros looked back steadily, and Matthew could see that he was totally serious. He looked beyond Kuros to see that the walls of their tiny room were drawing ever closer. A truth, huh? Well, it was worth a try.

Matthew thought quickly. "Okay, here goes," he said. "Last year in Mrs. O'Donnell's pre-algebra class I cheated on a test. Well, I didn't cheat on the *whole* test — I just sneaked one little look at Scott Downey's paper. Just for the answer to one little question." Matthew paused. Kuros was still gazing at him, as steadily as ever.

"Well, the thing is," he continued, "I think that one right answer might have been the whole reason I got a *B* instead of a *C* in that class. And because I kept a *B* average, my parents gave me a skateboard for my birthday."

Kuros nodded. He couldn't have had the faintest notion of what Matthew was talking about, but he seemed to understand. "And here is my truth," he said. "I am too often full of pride and vanity. I find myself stopping at pools in the forest, in order to admire my reflection. I spend hours polishing my armor so that it will gleam brighter than the other knights'."

Matthew now had his turn to nod understandingly. He'd probably be vain, too, if he looked like Kuros. Just to have biceps like his . . . Suddenly Matthew noticed that the room seemed to be growing brighter. In fact, the room was growing! The walls were pulling away from Matthew and Kuros.

"And now," said Kuros. "Quickly. Tell me a good deed you will perform. But promise nothing unless you intend to do it, my squire."

Matthew had no trouble figuring that one out. "As soon as I get back — I mean, *if* I get back, I'll go see Mrs. O'Donnell and tell her what I did. If she wants to change my permanent record, she can. And I'll do odd jobs in the neighborhood and earn enough money to pay my parents back for the skateboard. And . . . "

"That's enough," said Kuros. "And I, in turn, will do my best to avoid vanity in the future." He looked down at himself ruefully. "Though I think it will not be difficult, judging by my appearance these days."

Matthew laughed. It was true that Kuros was looking a little dog-eared. His armor was dented and scratched, and his flowing hair was a bird's nest of tangles. And then, Matthew saw something behind Kuros. A tunnel had opened up in the wall of their blue prison.

"All *right!*" he yelled. He took off down the corridor, with Kuros right behind him. He had no idea where they were headed. He only knew that he wanted to get away from where they'd been.

They soon slowed to a walk as they again followed the twists and turns of the blue caves. Once again they came to a fork in the tunnels; once again they decided by whim which way to go. It was clear that they were still lost.

It seemed like they had walked for hours when Matthew looked ahead in the distance to see a red glow. It didn't look like daylight, exactly, but any color other than blue was a welcome sight. Matthew and Kuros broke into a run toward the glow.

It was a chest, a glowing red chest. Matthew was a little disappointed — he'd been hoping the glow would have something to do with a way out of the blue caves. He'd been imagining a giant red arrow, with a neon sign below it that read THIS WAY OUT. But it was only a chest.

Kuros seemed disappointed, too. He gave the chest a little kick with the Boots of Force, but the chest wouldn't open. "I thought not," he said. "We would need a key for this one, and we'll never find a key in this maze."

A smile spread over Matthew's face as he dug into his pocket. Kuros grinned back when he caught sight of the gleaming red key in Matthew's hand.

The key fit perfectly into the lock, but when the chest yawned open, Matthew felt let down yet again. There was no weaponry, no special boots or shield. There weren't even any gems in the chest. Just some old piece of paper, rolled up and tied with a gold ribbon.

Matthew was about to let the lid of the chest fall, but Kuros stopped him and reached in to grab the paper.

It was a map. A map of the whole land of Elrond, with a YOU ARE HERE arrow pulsing next to a small red chest deep in the heart of the Blue Caves.

Matthew and Kuros looked at the map, and then at each other. A map. They were saved! Matthew would be able to apologize to Mrs. O'Donnell after all.

This called for more than just a high five. Matthew taught Kuros how to do a secret handshake that he and his friends had made up. It started with a couple of high fives, then a couple of low fives and a hip check. It ended with elbow touches. Then they looked at the map.

Their way out was clear. But Matthew saw Kuros shudder when he saw what they would face when they finally emerged from the Blue Caves. "I have heard tales of the FireWorld, ever since I was small, " said the knight. "It was the place parents threatened to send their misbehaving children — a land of lava and flaming coals."

"We'll never get through FireWorld without the Boots of Lava Walk," said Kuros. "We must find them. We'll have to give up the Boots of Force for them, but we must have them."

Matthew and Kuros set out, newly confident, with the map held in front of them. Two rights, a left, and another sharp right brought them to a large blue cavern. A niche was carved into the far wall, and sitting within it was a glowing green potion in a small glass bottle. Kuros strode to the ledge, grabbed the bottle, and took a sip of the potion.

Matthew was shaking his head disgustedly — didn't Kuros have *any* common sense? — when he stopped to stare in disbelief. Kuros was suddenly hovering several feet above the ground.

"A wonderful potion, my squire!" said Kuros from where he floated. "The Potion of Levitation. Have some?"

Matthew thought it looked like fun, floating like that, but he turned down the offer. He still didn't like the idea of just drinking down any old potion you came across. "No thanks, Kuros. I'd rather keep my feet on solid ground," he said.

Just then, a bat flew by Matthew's head, so close that he could feel the breeze it stirred up. And then another bat — and another. The cavern was suddenly full of bats. They dove and swooped, baring tiny — but extremely sharp-looking — teeth.

"Watch out, Squire!" called Kuros. "I've heard of these bats. Their bite is poison, and Malkil has trained them to attack. No one knows if a traveler like you could be hurt by them." Then there was no more conversation, as Kuros went to work.

The Potion of Levitation proved its worth as Kuros hovered in the air, then came to earth, then rose again. The Dagger of Throwing was a steely blur as Kuros fought off the bats.

Matthew stood to one side, wishing as usual that he could join the battle. He did what he could be warning Kuros of bats behind him and by yelling "Jump!" when he felt that some Levitation might come in handy.

The battle was intense, but it was over soon. Kuros stood panting, looking glad to be on solid ground. The dagger fell to the ground from his tired fingers. It struck the ground with a strange, hollow clunk.

"Clunk?" Matthew looked at the spot where the dagger had fallen. Why did it make a noise at all, if it was just falling into the dirt? He ran to sweep the dirt away. There was a chest here, half buried in the dirt. And it was a gray chest, which meant that the Boots of Force should open it.

Kuros regained his energy when he saw the chest, and set to work with Matthew, digging it out. Before long, the chest sat on the ground. It was covered with dirt and grime, as were Matthew and Kuros by now. Kuros looked it over, then aimed one good hard kick at the most likely spot. The chest opened immediately.

Inside lay a pair of boots. They were made of leather, but they shone like gold. The cuffs were trimmed with diamonds, which glinted blue in the light of the caves. Kuros smiled. "Luck has graced us again, my squire. Behold the Boots of Lava Walk."

Kuros looked down at the crimson Boots of Force, still on his feet. It was clear that he'd become attached to them. "I think that this red suits me better. Do you not agree?" he asked.

Matthew looked at him as though he were crazy. "I thought you said that we *had* to have these boots, for FireWorld!" he said. Then he realized that Kuros was joking with him — pretending to still be consumed by vanity.

Matthew helped Kuros off with the Boots of Force, and into the Boots of Lava Walk. Kuros stamped around in them for a moment, and seemed satisfied with the fit. Matthew almost laughed aloud, thinking that Kuros looked just like some guy in a shoe store, checking out his new shoes.

It was short work from that point to follow the map to the very edge of the caves. Matthew could see ahead to where yellow daylight cast a strange color onto the blue walls of the cave, when Kuros called a halt.

There, tied to a stalagmite, was a girl, dressed in a blue gown. She had bright red hair and a sprinkle of freckles across her nose. She wasn't as beautiful as Lucinda, but she had a spunky look in her eye that Matthew liked.

"Ahem," said the girl. "My name is Esmerelda. Are you planning to rescue me? Or should I wait for the *next* knight?"

Matthew's jaw dropped. This one was a real wise guy. Or would that be a wise damsel?

Once they'd untied her, Esmerelda turned out to be just as grateful as Lucinda had been. And, like Lucinda, she gave them a few tips about what lay ahead.

"I see you've got the Boots of Lava Walk," she finished. "You'll need them. And now, I bid you farewell." She kissed Matthew on the cheek, which made him blush feverishly. Then she took a few steps down the path in front of them.

Matthew watched closely this time. He saw her dress turn white, and then she disappeared, just as Lucinda had. A twinkle of light marked her departure.

Matthew sank against the cavern wall. These damsels were too much. Suddenly, the wall gave way, and Matthew fell backward into another tunnel. This tunnel wasn't blue. It was *red*, as in red-hot.

GAME HINT

The gray doors don't require a key.

Chapter Nine

Hot. It was so hot. Hotter than anything Matthew had ever felt before. Hotter than a heat wave in August. Hotter than the bonfire at the skating rink on a cold December day. Hotter than a pizza right out of the oven at Sal's Pizzeria.

Matthew tumbled and fell, aware of nothing but the heat. He wasn't really scared, or panicked, or even nervous. He almost felt like he could just fall asleep, take a nap in the incredible heat. It was like those people who got lost in blizzards and curled up in snowbanks and went to sleep, only to freeze to death. Only there was no snow here — just heat.

Flames licked out at him as he fell, singeing his eyelashes. Ouch! He was supposed to be completely safe here. It seemed that the closer he got to Malkil, the more danger he was in. Matthew blinked. A thought began to work its way into his brain. What was going to happen when he hit bottom? What would the bottom be like? He could bet it wasn't going to be pleasant. In fact, this could really be the end of the line. What would happen if he actually died in Elrond? Would he just disappear entirely from his own world? His parents would never know what had happened to him.

Now Matthew was beginning to feel afraid. He was even beginning to panic a little. But what could he do? How could he save himself? The heat pressed on him, surrounding him entirely. Matthew just kept falling.

And then, he landed. Not on a bed of coals, not in a river of lava, but into the arms of Kuros. Matthew had almost forgotten that Kuros existed, but here he was. The knight stood steady as a rock, cradling Matthew in his arms as if he were a baby. Matthew's whole body just sagged in relief. He was safe.

But he wasn't a baby. And he suddenly felt pretty silly lying there in Kuros's arms. He struggled to get down, but Kuros tightened his hold. "Wait, my squire," he said. "Look!"

Kuros was pointing to the ground. Matthew looked down, but there was no "ground" to be seen. There was just lava. And not a river of lava, either. This was an *ocean* of lava. Red-gold streams and pools and fountains and lakes of bubbling, molten lava. Matthew stopped trying to get down.

"But how...?" How was Kuros able to stand there so calmly? It was impossible. Nobody could withstand such heat.

"It's the boots, Squire. The boots!" Kuros was elated. "They really work. Malkil is doing his best to cook us alive, but the boots will save us."

Matthew looked down at Kuros's feet. Sure enough, the Boots of Lava Walk were the only thing standing between Kuros and a major case of the hotfoots. "Awesome," Matthew whispered.

"Truly," answered Kuros. "Now, get onto my back so that we may be on our way."

Matthew clambered awkwardly over the knight's massive body until he was in "piggyback" position on Kuros's back. Kuros began to walk, picking his way through the simmering pools and dodging the huge lava bubbles that broke free and rose from the main mass. It was slow going.

Suddenly, Matthew realized that he was thirsty. Very thirsty. He thought about a tall glass of ice water. He thought about a cold can of ginger ale. He thought about a 2-liter bottle of Coke. He swallowed and tried to stop thinking.

Kuros trudged on. Geysers of flame spurted out of the lava, almost knocking him over. Matthew tightened his grip until Kuros made a choking sound.

Matthew looked up to see a bat coming toward them, winging its evil way through the flames. Its teeth were bared. "Kuros!" He cried. But how could the knight fight off the nasty creature? If he let go of Matthew, Matthew would fall into the lava.

Kuros looked up in time to see the bat. "The dagger, Squire. Take it and throw well!"

Matthew didn't stop to think. He reached down and grabbed the dagger from its little sheath at Kuros's side. He held it and aimed it at the oncoming bat. And he let it fly. It flew crookedly, and it didn't hit the bat straight on. But it stopped the bat for a moment.

It stopped the bat long enough for Kuros to rearrange his grip on Matthew, grab the dagger as it returned from its flight, and throw it again. This time the bat fell shrieking into the lava.

"Good work, Squire!" said Kuros.

"Thanks," said Matthew. But the tone in Kuros's voice reminded him of something. It was just like baseball practice, when he would grab onto, but not quite catch, a hard grounder hit to him at second base. "Nice stop," Coach Miles would say, in exactly the same tone of voice Kuros had used. Well, he'd probably never be a Yankee. And he sure wasn't ready for knighthood, either.

"I don't think you could have slain him, in any case," said Kuros. "Remember, you are of another world. And he was one of Malkil's enchanted minions."

Matthew cheered up a little. After all, he

had helped out, even if he hadn't destroyed the enemy totally. But this FireWorld was no fun. It was just plain too hot to stand for long. "Kuros, we've got to figure out a way to move faster," he said. "After all, we've got the map. We know where we're going, right? So let's *go!*"

"I, too, wish to hurry," said Kuros. "But these boots were not built for speed."

Matthew thought. He looked around, and thought some more. Then, out of the corner of his eye, he saw a lava bubble, an enormous one, just floating along about three feet above the surface of the lava. "Kuros!" he yelled. "Jump onto that bubble!"

Kuros flinched. Matthew realized that he'd shouted right into the knight's ear. But there was no time to lose. "Now!" He yelled again, "Jump!"

"Surely you jest, Squire," said Kuros. "We cannot ride a bubble as though it were a horse."

"No, but we can ride it like a skateboard," Matthew said. "Just get on, and then I'll teach you."

With some difficulty, Kuros managed to get both of them onto the bubble. He stood swaying, about to topple over and dump them into the boiling lava.

"Crouch down a little," said Matthew. He'd never skateboarded piggyback before. This would be a challenge. "Now, spread your feet apart some, and shift around until you find your balance."

Kuros was concentrating hard. The lava bubble kept sailing along, twisting and turning wildly under its new weight.

"Put your arms out if you need some help balancing," said Matthew. He tightened his hold on Kuros's shoulders. "You got it!" he cried as Kuros stopped wobbling and the bubble's path straightened out. "All right!"

Kuros turned his head so that Matthew could see the gigantic grin he wore. "Squire, this is astounding!" he said. "You have invented a wonderful new way to travel."

Matthew didn't correct him. Who *had* invented the skateboard, anyway? Well, it looked like the history books in Elrond would list Matthew Lukens. No matter. It just felt great to be riding again.

Chapter Ten

Matthew was almost getting used to the heat. They'd gotten beyond the main lava flow now, and had entered a network of caverns. Flames roared and flickered up the walls of the caves, and pools of lava were dotted here and there. But Matthew and Kuros were able to walk again, as long as they chose their path carefully.

Kuros looked as if the heat were really getting to him. All that armor can't be helping, thought Matthew. The knight was gasping for air as he picked his way through the cavern.

"The keys," he said, panting. "We must find the keys." He stumbled forward.

Matthew ran his eyes around the walls of the cave. He'd had good luck before by looking on ledges, checking every nook and cranny.

Nothing. He raised his gaze to the ceiling, wishing that they could be finished with FireWorld.

There, on a high, high ledge, he spied just the tip of what looked like a key. A red key. "Kuros, look!" he said. "Up there." He pointed.

Kuros looked, and shook his head. "We'll have to do without that one," he said. "I can't climb those walls."

"What about the potion?" Matthew asked. The heat must really be slowing down Kuros's thinking. "The Potion of Levitation."

Kuros nodded and pulled the tiny flask from an inner pocket. He sipped, and immediately rose to the ceiling. "A little too much," he called down to Matthew. He waited until the potion began to wear off, and as he began to descend he grabbed the key from its ledge.

"Got it," he said. "Now all we have to do is find the chest it opens." He tucked the key into a pocket. "Let's check the map and see which way we should be heading."

Kuros pulled out the map, unrolled it, and knelt to examine it.

Just then, Matthew saw something horrible. It was a skull, hovering in the air behind Kuros. A huge, grinning skull. Matthew tried to yell out, to warn the knight. "K-k-k-k!" He couldn't talk. Another skull appeared next to the first one. This was awful!

"Kuros!" There, he'd finally gotten it out.

"What is it, my squire?" asked Kuros.

"Look, here is our next destination. We are not far from the Pink Caves now."

"Kuros, a sk— sk— sk—" Oh, man, now he couldn't get out the next word. Another skull joined the first two. Their grins widened. Matthew felt like they were laughing at him.

Malkil. It was all Malkil's work. And these skulls were nothing to be afraid of— they were just apparitions created by the evil wizard. Matthew drew himself up and moved toward Kuros — and toward the skulls.

The skulls suddenly grouped into formation and swooped down upon the unsuspecting Kuros, chattering their teeth as they flew at him. Kuros threw up his hands to ward them off. Matthew darted in to grab BrightSword, which had been lying on the ground next to Kuros. He shoved the weapon into the knight's hand, and Kuros went into action.

Matthew loved the sound of BrightSword at work. *Whup-whup-whup!* The steel just sang as it whipped through the air, reflecting the dull red glow of FireWorld.

Before long, Kuros stood in the center of a pile of broken bones. Skulls lay in pieces all around him. He sheathed BrightSword and leaned against the wall. "More of Malkil's beings," he said. "The wizard must know that we are drawing closer to his lair."

Matthew wasn't sure he was all that eager to come face-to-face with Malkil. A mind that could dream up those skulls ... not to mention the poisonous bats. This was not a friendly guy.

With his mind still on Malkil, Matthew led the way through the flame-filled cavern. The heat of this world never seemed to let up. Matthew felt like he was roasting. "Just like a burger on the grill," he said aloud.

Kuros didn't respond. He just trudged along behind Matthew, occasionally wiping the sweat from his eyes.

"I am *so* thirsty," Matthew went on. He waited for Kuros's question, but when it didn't come, he supplied it himself. "How thirsty *are* you, Matthew?" He went for the joke now, feeling lightheaded in the heat. "I'm so thirsty that . . ." but the punch line for that one would have to wait. Matthew suddenly had better things to do than act like a stand-up comedian.

There, not one hundred yards in front of him, was a pool. A superdeluxe, built-in, turquoise-water, two-diving-boards *pool*. Next to the pool was a little patio, and on the patio was a little round table with an umbrella over it and two chairs beside it. On the table sat an enormous pitcher of — was that lemonade? — and two tall, frosty glasses.

Matthew took off toward the pool, pulling his shirt over his head as he ran. *"Yaaa-hooooo!"* he cried. He knew just how that cool water was going to feel on his hot, dusty skin. He ran faster.

And then, he stopped short. Something

had grabbed him from behind. "Hey!" he said. "Are you nuts? What do you think you're doing?" Kuros was holding Matthew back. He'd grabbed him by the waistband of his jams, and he wasn't letting go. "Haven't you ever seen a pool before? C'mon! I'll teach you how to do a cannonball. Let *go!*"

"Squire. Squire! Listen to me. There's nothing there. It's a trick. Malkil's trick. Stop. Look." Kuros spoke gently, but firmly.

Matthew stopped struggling and looked toward the pool. The turquoise water shimmered, wavered, and . . . disappeared. The patio with its table disappeared. The two diving boards disappeared. Where they'd been there was now a huge, boiling lake of molten lava.

As Matthew watched in horror, the lava moved and shifted until it was in the shape of a face — an unspeakably evil face. "That's Malkil!" said Kuros.

Matthew could hardly stand to look. Then the lava shifted again and the face was gone.

"Never fear, Squire. Malkil is only trying to slow us down. But we must keep moving! We must get out of here soon," said Kuros. "Look! I think Malkil was using an illusion to distract us from that." He pointed toward the back of the cavern, away from where the "pool" had been.

Matthew looked, and saw a red chest, glowing amid the fiery embers. As they approached it, Kuros pulled the red key they'd found from his pocket. "Go ahead, Squire," he said. "You open it." Matthew knew that Kuros was trying to make him feel better and forget about the pool. It wasn't working, but he appreciated the gesture.

"Thanks," he said, turning the key in the lock. The chest opened to reveal the nastiest-looking weapon Matthew had ever seen. This was no little dagger. It was an ax, and it looked big enough to chop down a redwood. Matthew bent down and tried to lift it out of the chest. *"Unnngh!"* He couldn't budge the thing.

Kuros reached in and lifted it out. It looked like it belonged in his huge, muscled arms. He cradled it happily. "The Ax of Agor. Now *this* is a weapon. We'll need this as we fight our way into the castle. Now I feel ready for anything." He slammed the chest closed. "Let's go!" He slung the ax over his shoulder and led the way.

As they turned the corner into the last cavern of FireWorld, Matthew heard shrieks. He looked up. It was another damsel. She was wearing a long red dress. She was chained to a rock. And there was a river of molten lava flowing toward that rock, picking up speed every second. No wonder she was shrieking.

Kuros and Matthew charged toward the rock. Matthew introduced himself as Kuros tried out his new ax on the chains. Galadriel turned out to be just as smart and nice as the other damsels. And, like the others, she disappeared before Matthew really had a chance to get to know her. The last he saw of her was a view from the back, as her red dress turned to white. He sighed.

"On to the Pink Caves," shouted Kuros gleefully.

"Right," said Matthew wearily. "On to the Pink Caves."

GAME HINT

To fight the ghost, use your Cloak of Darkness to become invisible.

Chapter Eleven

"These caves don't look so pink to me," said Matthew. They had passed through the last cavern of FireWorld and entered another cavern. The heat was finally over, and it was a relief. Now they stood in a grim, gray world. Gray walls, gray ceiling, gray floor. Matthew shivered. This place felt cold and dank and . . . dead.

"Methinks we have some battle to do before we enter the Pink Caves," said Kuros. "This looks like the lair of Rockface." He turned around warily, looking for his enemy. Then he unbuckled the belt from which hung BrightSword's sheath.

"Squire, I will ask you to hold this for me. BrightSword will be of no use against this foe." He handed the sword to Matthew.

Suddenly, one of the walls seemed to

burst into life. It was just like in that movie *Alien,* thought Matthew. A huge, rocklike figure rushed at Kuros with a sound like thunder. Matthew saw Kuros stumble, then regain his balance.

The creature swung at Kuros with heavy fists, moving forward without pause. Kuros was pushed backward until his back was against the wall. Matthew looked closely at the knight's face. He wasn't smiling this time. In fact, he looked almost afraid.

And then Kuros's face changed. He held the Ax of Agor high, and smashed it down upon the rocky body of his opponent. Finally, Rockface was slowed. But the creature recovered quickly and came in for another attack on Kuros.

The Ax of Agor swung and swung again. Matthew could see that each blow was a tremendous effort for Kuros. Pieces of rock flew off the knight's attacker and smashed into the cavern walls. Matthew flattened himself into a corner.

"Matthew!" called Kuros, grunting with effort. "Look for the door! We must find the entrance to the Pink Caves."

Matthew looked around wildly. He hadn't noticed any doors in this cave at all. But then he saw it. A gray door, set unobtrusively into the cavern wall. And it was clear that Rockface was guarding it. There was no way he was about to let them get through.

"Kuros!" Matthew yelled. When he had the knight's attention, he pointed at the door. Kuros nodded and kept on swinging the ax. Rockface seemed invincible. Matthew put his hands over his ears to try to block out the creature's thunderous roaring.

And then it was quiet. One mighty swing of the ax had felled the monstrous foe. Kuros turned to Matthew. "Quickly, Squire. Through the door!"

They ran for the door, and Matthew put his shoulder against it to push it open. Just then, he heard something behind him. It wasn't as loud as Rockface's roar. It sounded like the noise in a bowling alley, with balls rolling and pins falling. He turned around.

Where the body of Rockface had fallen were now hundreds of smaller creatures, tiny versions of their demolished parent. They swarmed at Kuros and Matthew.

Kuros swung the ax, destroying several enemies with each blow. It was clear that the knight was tiring, though. The ax was a heavy weapon.

Matthew slipped into position by Kuros's side and helped the knight trade weapons. BrightSword would take care of these smaller Rockfaces. The creatures ignored Matthew, as all of Malkil's beings did. But Matthew did not feel entirely safe until Kuros had finished off the last of them with the Dagger of Throwing.

Finally, Kuros stood triumphant amid the bodies of his opponents. But Matthew knew there was no time to lose. They must move on. He grabbed the knight's arm and pulled him through the gray door.

Chapter Twelve

The Pink Caves. Finally. Matthew looked around. Well, they were pink, that was true. But what he hadn't expected was the cold. The Rockface's lair had been cool, but the Pink Caves were downright freezing.

Matthew let out a breath and saw the cloud it made, glowing softly pink in the light of the caves. He shivered, and folded his arms over his chest. He'd thought that the Pink Caves might be kind of pleasant compared to some of the places he'd been, but now his hopes were dashed.

The Pink Caves were just as nasty as the rest of Malkil's worlds. They were cold and unrelentingly pink, and full of the threat of evil. "I don't understand, Kuros," said Matthew. "What's so great about the Pink Caves? You were so eager to get here."

"It is true, Squire, that these caves are not pleasant," said Kuros. But I have reason to be glad that we are here." He paused. "I believe that my sister, Grizelda, is one of the damsels that Malkil captured, and my heart tells me that she is imprisoned in these very caves."

Grizelda! Matthew tried not to show what he was thinking. With a name like Grizelda, she couldn't be much to look at. But if she was Kuros's sister, he'd be glad to help rescue her. After all, looks weren't everything. "We'd better get going," he said. He led the way deeper into the cavern.

"I curse the fates that took a low-born girl and turned her into a lady-in-waiting to a princess," said Kuros, as he walked along next to Matthew. "And I blame myself. If I hadn't wanted so badly to be a knight, perhaps she would have been content herself to remain a miller's daughter."

"How *did* you get to be a knight?" asked Matthew. "I kind of thought you had to be a rich guy to be a knight."

"I offered myself as squire to one of the prince's men," said Kuros. I worked with him for many years, taking care of his horses, cleaning his armor, and caring for his weapons. He was a good master, but the work was hard." Kuros sighed, remembering.

"Most of the other squires were high-born lads, who would be dubbed by the king and become knights when they reached the age of twenty. But a miller's son does not often get dubbed by the king."

"So how did you get to be a knight?" asked Matthew persistently.

"One day I rode with my knight into a terrific battle. It was a clamorous, bloody fight, and we were greatly outnumbered." Kuros's eyes gleamed as he remembered the battle. "My knight shouted to me as we fought side by side. 'Be thou a knight,' he cried. And that was *my* dubbing. No ceremony, no special red cloak, no king, no feasting. I was dubbed on the field of battle, and I am proud of it."

Matthew nodded. What a great story! "What about Grizelda?" he asked.

"She came to watch me fight in a tournament one day," said Kuros. "For some reason, she caught the prince's eye, and he pressed his sister to take her into service. From that day onward she was part of the court."

Matthew figured the prince must be half blind — or half crazy — to fall for someone named Grizelda, but he held his tongue. The whole story was pretty neat, anyway. He looked around at the central cavern they'd come to while they talked.

Pink ice coated the walls of the huge room, and icicles hung down like stalactites. Matthew's hands were freezing. The cold seemed to penetrate right to his bones. It was an evil cold.

Kuros was walking around the edges of the cavern, searching for keys that they might need on their journey. Matthew joined him, checking out likely crevices and searching for niches where keys might be hidden. "Kuros, where do you think Grizelda is being held?" he asked, as he poked his hand into a crevice.

"Yikes!" he cried. Something — or somebody — had chomped down on his hand. He pulled it out quickly, looking to see if the skin had been broken. He was supposed to be safe! A tiny skull was latched onto his little finger. He shook his hand wildly, trying to get rid of it. A bigger skull flew out of the crevice. "Kuros! Help!" Finally the little skull let go and flew toward Kuros.

The knight grabbed the dagger from its sheath and threw it again and again as two more, then ten more skulls flew out of their hiding places in the walls.

Matthew went back to the crevice where he'd first been bitten. That skull must have been guarding something. It took a while for him to work up the courage to put his hand into the crevice again, but when he finally did he was rewarded. He was right! There was a key in there.

He turned to check on Kuros. He was fighting wildly, surrounded by skulls now. Their wild chattering filled the cave, echoing off the walls. The dagger flashed, and skulls fell left and right. Despite the apparent mayhem, Kuros remained in control.

Matthew continued around the cavern walls, checking each of the crevices from which he'd seen a skull fly out. Soon a collection of keys made a satisfying jingle in his pocket. And then the cave was quiet. Kuros had destroyed every last skull.

GAME HINT

To beat the little guy, jump over him, hit him, then jump over him again. Levitate to pick up all your points.

Chapter Thirteen

The quiet felt wonderful, but somehow Matthew didn't think it was going to last. He had the feeling that this cold, evil cave was full of enemies. "Let's keep going, Kuros," he said to the exhausted knight. "We've got to find Grizelda."

Kuros nodded and sheathed the dagger. Matthew waited as Kuros stepped gingerly over the pile of skulls that lay on the floor and picked his way through a row of stalagmite icicles.

They started walking again, but they'd only gone two or three steps before a swarm of bats appeared out of nowhere, baring their sharp teeth as they swooped down to attack Kuros. Again, Matthew was ignored.

He could only yell directions as Kuros thrust BrightSword and then switched to the dagger, destroying several bats with each throw. By the time they were all finished off,

Kuros was dripping with sweat. In the cold air of the caves, the steam rose from his shoulders.

"Malkil knows we draw near," said Kuros, panting. "He will not hold back any of his helpers from this point on."

Matthew was worried. How was Kuros going to keep up with all of these attacks? It was true that the knight was an incredible warrior, but how much could he take? It was so frustrating that he couldn't help in any real way.

Matthew looked around to get his bearings. Which way had they been headed? Then he saw it. One of the stalagmites was glowing — a bright, white glow in the midst of all that pink.

He walked over to it and looked more closely. It didn't look exactly like the other stalagmites — it wasn't as lumpy, or as pointed on the end. It looked more like some kind of a staff. He looked back at Kuros. The knight seemed to be resting for a moment, gathering his strength.

Matthew reached out carefully and touched the stalagmite. It broke off into his hand, and glowed even brighter. Now he was frightened. Was this one of Malkil's enchantments? He turned to ask Kuros, and saw that the knight was on his way over. Then, without any warning, Kuros froze in his tracks.

"Kuros! What is it?" asked Matthew. Kuros didn't answer. He stood stock-still, looking like he'd been carved out of ice. What had happened? Matthew was suddenly very frightened. What was he doing here, in the midst of these bizarre pink caves, in the middle of a country he'd never heard of? He dropped the glowing staff and ran toward Kuros.

As quickly as he'd become frozen, Kuros thawed. "What is it, Squire?" he asked.

Matthew was relieved. He went back to pick up the staff. He still didn't know what it was for, but maybe Kuros would. "Look what I found, Kuros!" he said.

"Zounds, Squire!" said Kuros. "It's the Wand of —" and suddenly he was frozen again.

Matthew was shaken. He'd been ready to forget the first time Kuros had frozen in position — some freak enchantment or something, he'd guessed — but now it was happening again. They'd never find Grizelda at this rate. And Princess Miranda was waiting. Sunset couldn't be all that far off. They didn't have time to waste.

He put the staff down again, carefully this time, and walked toward Kuros. The knight moved.

"What's going on?" said Matthew, bending to pick up the staff.

"Leave it!" shouted Kuros. "That is the Wand of Wonder that you have found. It freezes the motion of any being it is pointed toward." He laughed. "A wonderful weapon, but I would prefer that it be used against me no longer."

Matthew picked up the staff and examined it. "You mean that's why you were frozen? Because I pointed this at you? All right!" He thought that the wand was a pretty cool weapon. It reminded him of that game he used to play when he was a little kid — Statues. When you were "it," you spun the other kids around and then let them fly. They had to stay frozen in the position they'd landed in.

But this was no game. And the wand was no toy. He handed it to Kuros. "Here, you take it," he said. "Just don't freeze *me*, okay?"

It wasn't long before Kuros had a chance to try out the wand on a screaming horde of flying spiders. It worked even better than their old cuckoo clock had, back in the forest. The spiders hung frozen in space, and Kuros and Matthew stepped calmly through their midst. The spiders had been guarding a gray door.

"Here we come, Grizelda!" shouted Kuros, putting his shoulder to the door. But when they tumbled through the opening, all they found was a small, glowing red chest, and when Matthew checked his pockets they found that one of the keys he'd been saving fit the lock perfectly.

"Aha!" said Kuros, when he saw the contents. Matthew saw a blur of beautiful tapestry as Kuros pulled a cloak out of the chest and put it on. Then Matthew saw . . . nothing. Kuros had disappeared.

Matthew spun around. Where was Kuros? It wasn't comfortable to be suddenly alone in this dismal gray cave. And what was that sound? Oh, no! A swarm of chattering ghosts appeared out of nowhere, surrounding Matthew. He tried to beat the ghosts off with his arms, but he had little effect on them. He could feel their cold presence all around him. The closer Matthew came to Malkil, the less invulnerable he felt. The ghosts were closing in on him!

And then, they began to disappear, one by one, shrieking as they felt the dagger. "I am here, Squire," said Kuros from nearby. "I wear the Cloak of Darkness."

Matthew looked closely at the spot where he'd heard Kuros's voice, but he could see nothing. The ghosts had clearly found the knight, though, as they swarmed over him, trying to dodge his blade as they attacked.

Soon Matthew learned to follow Kuros's progress by watching the ghosts fall as Kuros cut a swath through their numbers. This Cloak of Darkness was a great find!

Once the ghosts had been taken care of, Kuros came back into view. Matthew had to admit he was relieved to see the knight again. "Now," said Kuros. "Back through that door. We must find Grizelda."

They retraced their steps and reentered the cold Pink Caves. It wasn't long before they rounded a curve to see a group of the ugliest beings Matthew had ever seen.

"Malkil's Goblins," said Kuros in a hushed voice. "Take care. They are as mean as they are unsightly."

They approached the hideous little creatures quietly. The tallest one had a long, crooked nose, and stood about two feet tall. Kuros donned the cloak and readied the Wand of Wonder. The circle of goblins parted as they heard approaching footsteps, and Matthew saw that they guarded a damsel. Her back was turned to Matthew, and her long brown hair tumbled down over a pink gown.

"Grizelda!" Kuros cried. She turned at the sound of his voice, and Matthew's knees melted. Suddenly he believed in love at first sight. He knew then that Grizelda was the most beautiful name he'd ever heard. Grizelda. Grizelda. The name would haunt his dreams.

"Untie her, Squire! Why do you delay?" Kuros was busy freezing the horrific goblins with his wand. The creatures stood still in frightening poses, teeth bared and sharp claws at the ready.

Matthew wove between them and loosened the knots that held Grizelda to the stalagmite. When she had been freed, she threw her arms around Matthew. He stood frozen, not knowing exactly what to do. Should he hug her back?

"Oh, thank you! Thank you!" she cried. "Those repulsive creatures were discussing whether to have me for breakfast or for lunch." She loosened her grip on Matthew and stepped back. "But you are not Kuros. I heard his voice, I know it. Where is my dear brother?"

Kuros threw off the cloak and ran to her. They hugged and kissed, and Matthew saw tears fall from their eyes. He felt a little choked up himself.

"And now you go to do battle with Malkil." she said. "I will come with you."

Matthew's heart beat faster.

Kuros shook his head firmly. "I know you are handy with a crossbow, Sister, since I am the one who taught you. But our way is full of dangers and we have trouble enough with just the two of us."

Grizelda looked disappointed. Matthew was disappointed, too, but he knew that Kuros was right. He looked longingly at Grizelda.

She laughed. "Look at your squire, Brother," she said gaily. "I believe he would not mind my company." She walked to Matthew's side and kissed him on the cheek. "Fear not, good Squire. I know we shall meet again. Here, take this token and remember me as you do battle." She smiled and placed a small kiss on Matthew's cheek.

Matthew was speechless. He wanted to say something witty, or profound, or beautiful. Something she'd always remember. But he couldn't get a single word out. All he could do was watch as she kissed Kuros good-bye and skipped down the path.

When her dress turned white, he knew she'd be gone in a second. "Good-bye!" he called finally, giving her a wave. Oh, great, he thought. Real profound. She's probably forgotten me already. But I won't forget her for a long time.

Chapter Fourteen

Kuros pushed open a door set into a pink wall. Matthew stepped through the door, following the knight, and his heart sank. He could hardly believe his eyes. They were back in the forest.

Matthew groaned. "Oh, man," he said. "After all that, here we are back where we started." He looked around at the huge trees draped in vines. He groaned again.

"Fear not, Squire," said Kuros. "This is a different forest. Look, here on the map." He pulled out the parchment and unrolled it. "We are coming very close to Malkil's Castle IronSpire. Canst thou not feel the evil in this place?"

As soon as the knight spoke, Matthew knew it was true. This was a different forest. It looked, at first glance, just like the other one. But Kuros was right. This place almost *smelled* of evil.

It was darker in this forest, and it was even quieter than the other forest had been. The silence was so absolute that Matthew nearly jumped out of his skin when a wild shriek pierced the hush. "What was *that?*" he asked.

"Better not to know," answered Kuros grimly. "Let us move on. This is Malkil's domain, and it is best to go quickly through it."

Matthew glanced through the leaves, checking the position of the sun. It was much lower in the sky than when he'd last seen it. What if sundown came before they ever reached the castle?

Suddenly, Matthew felt an urgent need to hurry. It wasn't only Princess Miranda and the land of Elrond at stake anymore. If they were even a few minutes late, Grizelda would be lost to him forever, before he'd even had a chance to really get to know her.

Matthew followed the knight through the dense underbrush. He saw no birds or animals, but he couldn't shake the feeling that he was being watched by many pairs of eyes. He walked steadily forward, but he felt like every cell in his body was screaming at him to turn around and run the other way.

"We must seek keys here, Squire," said Kuros. "We will have need of them when we enter the castle."

Matthew nodded halfheartedly. Somehow he just didn't have the energy to climb trees and search the forest for keys. Did he really want to get into this castle? Every step brought him closer to Malkil.

"Tarry not, Squire," said Kuros. "Remember, we have a purpose. We must save Elrond. The princess awaits us, and her handmaidens."

Grizelda. Suddenly, Matthew thought again of her face, and how it had glowed in the pink light of the caves where he'd first seen her. He looked at Kuros. "Keys, " he said. "Let's find those keys!"

He led the way up the nearest tree, with Kuros behind him. They climbed, and searched, and climbed some more. They pocketed each key that they found, and the clink of the keys in his pocket kept Matthew's spirits high.

Before long, it seemed that news of their presence had spread through the forest. Malkil's creatures turned out in force. Kuros was attacked in turn by hordes of bats, swarms of hornets, armies of poison ants, and nests of spiders.

As usual, Matthew was totally ignored by the evil creatures. Kuros fought them off single-handedly, alternating expert throws of the dagger with thrusts of the Wand of Wonder. He hardly seemed bothered by the attacks. "There is much worse to come," he told Matthew. "Malkil keeps his most dangerous guardians close by him. These fiends are only meant to slow our approach so that he can prepare for our arrival."

Matthew shuddered. What would Malkil's "most dangerous guardians" be like? He thought he'd already seen some pretty nasty creatures. It was hard to imagine what could be worse.

And then, Matthew heard something. It was a sound so sweet, so beautiful and so pure — he could hardly believe his ears. What was a sound like that doing in this evil place?

It was the song of a bird.

The clear notes warbled and trilled, sounding like clear water spilling over rocks. Matthew looked up, and caught a glimpse of a wing as the bird flew off. He ran after it, following the delicious sound. Kuros followed behind. The bird flitted between the trees, singing as it traveled. At times it dipped low in its flight, so that Matthew could almost grab it. But then it would fly high again, as if daring Matthew to keep up.

This was not one of Malkil's illusions. Matthew was sure of it. This bird was a friend, in the midst of this friendless land. He trampled through the underbrush, following the bird. And then the bird stopped.

It perched in a branch at the very top of one of the tallest trees Matthew had yet seen. It sang some more, and the sound intoxicated Matthew. The bird looked as if it were planning to stay where it was for a while, and Matthew began to figure out how to climb up to it.

It would be a treacherous climb, but Matthew felt that he must get closer to the bird. Its song was beautiful — it reminded him of Grizelda. He looked the tree over. Although it was not a species that he'd ever seen before — none of the trees in Elrond were familiar to him — it did remind him of the giant spruce in his front yard.

Both trees had a similar shape — like a Christmas tree — and both had branches that grew in a way that made them pretty easy to climb. Matthew started out. It was going to be a long climb.

Kuros stood below, watching. Matthew waved at him from the branch he stood on, and kept on climbing.

Soon his hands were smeared with sticky sap, and his shirt was torn in more than one place. But the bird kept singing, and Matthew kept climbing. Kuros called encouragement from below.

Matthew squinted up through the branches that scratched his face. He was getting closer. The bird's song was sweeter than ever. He hauled himself up, grabbing at handholds and searching for secure spots to place his feet. He looked down. What a mistake!

He saw Kuros on the ground, far, far below. The knight looked tiny; in fact, he looked like the toy knight Matthew had found in his father's study, so long ago. Matthew let out a breath. This was so weird! What was he doing in the top of a tree the size of the Empire State Building, in the middle of an enchanted forest?

And then the bird sang again, and Matthew forgot everything except his mission: To get closer to the bird. He climbed some more. The sound grew closer. He pulled himself up onto one of the highest branches of the tree, and saw the bird. It was within his reach.

Matthew paused to gather his breath, and in that moment, the bird flew off in a flurry of feathers. Without thinking, Matthew reached out to grab one of them as they floated past him. He watched the bird fly away. It sang merrily as it disappeared into the distance. Matthew sighed.

What would he have done if he'd caught the bird, anyway, he thought. It was better off as it was, flying free through the forest and saving the place from being totally evil. Matthew looked at the feather he'd caught and decided it would make a good present for Grizelda. He put it in his pocket and started to climb back down to Kuros.

The climb went quickly. Matthew felt somehow lighter, less afraid of falling. He swung from each branch and instinctively found an easy path to the bottom. Kuros was waiting for him.

Matthew showed Kuros the feather, and Kuros grabbed it eagerly. "Squire!" he said excitedly. "This is—*ah-ah-achooo!*—the Feather of Feather Fall!" He rubbed his nose.

"This will — *ah-ah-achooo!* — be invaluable in our journey! It will help us — *ah-ah-achooooo!* — drift gently from — *aah-aah-mmmm* — caught that one — great heights!"

Matthew laughed. He couldn't help it. What a sight — the great and powerful knight conquered by a mere feather. "Why don't I carry that for you," he offered. "You seem to be a little bit allergic to it." As he put the feather in his pocket, Matthew heard a sound. It was like a reel of fishing line unwinding. *Zzzzzzzzzip!* He spun around to see what it was.

There, dropping down beside Kuros on a long thread of silk, was the hugest spider Matthew had ever seen. She was gigantic. The Queen Spider, thought Matthew.

The terrifying creature snapped at Kuros, waving her arms. She never even looked at Matthew, but he was used to that. Malkil's creatures never paid attention to him.

He could see that Kuros would have to fight this creature with speed and brains, not force. If he could get past her on a run, and then turn and fight . . .

"Run, Kuros!" yelled Matthew. "Run!"

Kuros turned. "I never run from danger," he said. Just then, the spider hit him from behind.

Chapter Fifteen

Kuros staggered. The bite had clearly been deep. He rocked back on his heels, then regained his balance and stood firm again. "Run!" Matthew yelled again, desperately. "Run over here, hit her, and run again! That's the only way you'll win!"

But Kuros ignored him and stood his ground. He drew BrightSword and got ready to thrust. But before he could make a move, the spider pounced again. Matthew saw her fangs sink deep into Kuros's arm. Just watching made him feel faint.

The spider hung on, injecting her poison. Kuros convulsed once, twice, three times. And then he fell and lay still.

Matthew ran to his side. Kuros did not move. The spider hung back, watching and waiting. Matthew felt sick. Was this the end of the knight? Had the warrior met his match?

Matthew grabbed Kuros's wrist and felt for a pulse. He couldn't feel anything. Oh, no. This couldn't be. Was Kuros truly dead? Matthew started to panic. Suddenly he felt completely alone in this evil land. How would he ever find his way home? And what about the quest? What about saving Elrond and the Princess Miranda? And . . . Grizelda?

And then another feeling washed over him. Grief. His friend Kuros was gone. His friend. Matthew had started this journey on a whim, but now he realized that Kuros had become one of the best friends he'd ever had. He bowed his head and wept, still holding Kuros's wrist in his hand.

What was that? He'd felt something. Just a little flutter. Was it a pulse? Could it be? "Kuros," he whispered. "Can you hear me, buddy?" The pulse beat again, stronger this time. It was as if Matthew were willing the knight, his friend, back to life.

Kuros moaned and shifted his position. Matthew grinned, and felt like cheering. Kuros was alive! The knight opened his eyes and looked straight at Matthew. "A thousand thanks, Squire," he said quietly. "I was gone, but you brought me back. My squire, my friend."

Matthew held out his hand and helped Kuros to his feet. He swayed for a moment and then regained his footing. Matthew could almost see the strength surging back into Kuros's body.

Kuros looked over at the Queen Spider. "Perhaps, my squire," he said to Matthew, "I will try it your way." Just then, the spider ran at him.

Kuros ran, whirled around, attacked with BrightSword, and ran again. He stopped short, whirled, and thrust once more. The spider dropped back, wounded. Kuros grinned at Matthew.

It was short work from there for Kuros to destroy the spider. Matthew watched as she met her fate, legs twitching madly until she fell still.

Kuros held his hand up wearily, asking for a high five. Matthew surprised himself by hugging the knight instead. Kuros stepped back at first, but then returned the embrace.

They broke apart at the sound of a faint voice. Matthew heard a distinct "Help!" He turned to look .

A girl was sitting nearby, at the base of a tree. "I'm Penelope," the girl said to him, in a soft, sweet voice. "The spider was guarding me. Can you help?" Matthew swallowed.

"Sure," he said. His heart belonged to Grizelda, but how could he walk away from pretty Penelope, who wore a long gown of the deepest brown velvet?

He held her hand reassuringly as Kuros cut away the spider's silk that bound her. When she was free, she squeezed his hand. "I thank you, Sire," she said. "You and your knight have rescued me from certain death. I wish you well in your journey, for surely you travel now to yon castle."

She waved her hand toward the edge of the forest. There, looming above the tallest trees, were the turrets of the Castle Iron-Spire.

"Please take every care, and do your best to rid this land of the evil man who rules it," she said. She squeezed Matthew's hand again, and walked away.

He watched as her dress turned to white and she disappeared behind a tree.

She had reminded him somehow of his mother. She wasn't nearly as old, of course, but there was just something so gentle about the way she'd held his hand. It was as if she knew somehow about all he'd come through to get to her. She knew how tired he was, and how afraid. Suddenly, Matthew missed his mom. He missed his dad, too, and his home, and his wonderful, messy old room.

Chapter Sixteen

Kuros looked closely at Matthew. Matthew realized that he must have sighed out loud.

"Thou art troubled, Squire," said Kuros. "Please tell me what is wrong."

"I guess I just feel a little homesick — I miss my parents," said Matthew. "And I've been gone so long. I bet they're worried to death about me."

"I miss my parents, too," said Kuros gently. "Listen. I know a way for you to see your mother and father and reassure yourself that they are well. Follow me."

Matthew shrugged and followed Kuros through the woods to a small clearing. In the middle of the clearing was a small, still pool surrounded by rocks. Kuros knelt by the pool, and Matthew crouched beside him.

"Look into the water, Squire," said Kuros. "Watch carefully."

Matthew leaned over to look into the pool. What had at first looked like still water was now swirling with cloudlike formations. Matthew stared as the clouds moved together and then parted to reveal a picture. At first the picture was out of focus, and then it cleared and Matthew gasped.

It was like looking at a TV screen: The picture was as real as life, and it was moving. And the picture was of Matthew's dad.

"Dad," said Matthew, under his breath. He could tell that his dad was still at work. Mr. Lukens puttered around the office, gathering work to take home and packing it into his briefcase, which sat on a chair. The scene was a familiar one to Matthew. He'd visited his dad's law office often.

Matthew saw all the details of the office he knew so well. There was the ashtray he'd made for his (nonsmoking) dad in kindergarten. Ugly old thing. And there was the picture of Matthew in his Little League outfit, the year his team had won the championship. And next to it was a picture of the whole family, sopping wet and grinning, taken after a rainstorm on their last camping trip.

Matthew felt very strange — happy and sad all at the same time. He wished he could reach right in and give his dad a hug, tell him that he was all right. But his dad didn't look too worried. How could that be? Didn't he somehow know that his son was in mortal danger?

"I guess it's better that he has no idea," said Matthew. Then, as he watched, the scene at the law office faded and another came into view. Again, he had to wait as the picture came into focus, and then, there she was. His mom.

She was at the museum, which wasn't unusual. She worked there. She was a curator, which meant that she decided what displays and exhibits the museum would have every year. She looked like she was checking out a new exhibit right now. Stuff was being unpacked from crates, and people were setting it up as she directed. Matthew looked closer.

It was an exhibit of arms and armor! He couldn't believe it. There were shields, and swords, and all kinds of chain mail. Mannequins were being dressed in full armor. One of them looked just like the Red Knight — except that the headpiece he wore was the wrong kind for the armor he was wearing. Matthew could hardly wait to get back and tell his mom so she could fix it.

Or maybe he wouldn't. How would his mom react if she heard about some of his adventures? She'd probably go nuts, never let him leave the house again!

What if she heard about the poison-fanged bats? The ghosts? What about the flowing lava in FireWorld? And forget about telling her about the Queen Spider. She'd probably pass out. No, it would be better if she never knew.

Matthew looked again at the exhibit she was setting up. He'd never been all that interested in her work before, but this stuff was cool. He'd have to check it out when he got back. And maybe he could go to the library and find some books on knights, too. It was all pretty interesting, once you started to know a little bit about it.

Matthew realized that he was thinking about doing all these things *when* he got back, not *if*. It was as if seeing his parents made him feel more connected to that life — his "real" life — and made him feel more optimistic about surviving his journey through Elrond.

But it also made him feel sad to see them. There they were, just going along as usual, with no idea of the grave danger he was in. They didn't even miss him! But he missed them. He missed them a lot, all of a sudden.

Kuros touched his arm gently. "The sun is low in the sky, Squire," he said. "The quest must continue."

Matthew took one more look at the scene. "Bye, Mom. Bye, Dad," he said softly. He turned away from the pool and wiped his eyes. Kuros clasped Matthew's shoulder.

"Matthew. You have been a brave companion and a great help to me so far on my quest," said the knight gravely. "You are valiant and true. If you wish to stop now and go back to your own world I will understand. Much danger lies ahead."

Matthew looked at the knight, and then looked beyond him at the turrets of the Castle IronSpire, rising above the edge of the forest. He paused for a moment.

"No, I can't go back. Not now," said Matthew. "Not when we've come so far. No way am I going to stop now!"

Kuros smiled. He held up his hand for a high five, and they ran through the secret handshake. Matthew glanced back once more at the pool, which was once more full of swirling clouds.

And then Kuros led the way, walking toward the huge castle that rose from the mists at the edge of the forest. The late evening sun glinted golden on its highest towers. They had no time to waste.

GAME HINT

Don't try to get past the Red Knight without the gems you need. You'll waste your time.

Chapter Seventeen

Matthew had never seen anything so big. Up close, the castle seemed to loom taller than the tallest skyscraper. It sprawled out sideways, too — it was like a whole city in one building.

Turrets and spires rose from all parts of the huge building, piercing the sky. Colorful banners flew from the battlements. The land surrounding the castle was landscaped into beautiful gardens, full of blossoming fruit trees. Graceful, long-necked white swans were swimming in the moat.

But the drawbridge was up. Every door in the castle was shut tight. And there was not a soul to be seen anywhere. No gardeners worked in the gardens. No knights patrolled the towers. No washerwomen hung out laundry. No dogs barked. Total silence reigned.

Matthew shuddered. He felt like he was being watched, even though there were no people visible. Were there archers peering out of the slits in the battlements, arrows at the ready? Or was it just Malkil, watching them approach his castle as he had watched them on their entire journey?

Then Matthew looked over at Kuros. The knight stared up at the castle, wide-eyed. He seemed frozen in place. He seemed ... frightened. Matthew was taken aback. Kuros afraid? This was new. And Kuros's fear made Matthew even more nervous. What were they getting into?

Then he gathered himself together. He'd have to help Kuros snap out of it. "So," he said. "How do we get in?"

"We cannot," said Kuros. "The castle is impregnable." He turned as if to walk away.

"Hey!" Matthew yelled. "Where do you think you're going?" There was only one explanation for Kuros's behavior. He must be falling under some kind of spell. One of Malkil's spells.

Matthew ran to Kuros's side and grabbed his arm. "Come on, buddy," he said. "We can't stop now. Look, we're just going to have to climb up the walls of the castle. Remember how you learned to climb trees? It'll be just like that."

Kuros gazed up at the immense castle and shook his head wearily. "I cannot," he said.

Matthew was beginning to panic. It was up to him to break this spell and get Kuros moving again. The sun was moments away from setting. Suddenly, he knew what to do. "Kuros," he said. "What about your mother and father? What about Grizelda? What about all of the good people of Elrond?"

The light began to come back into Kuros's eyes. Matthew continued. "What about Princess Miranda?"

"Miranda," Kuros sighed. "Miranda. I'm coming, my lady! Never fear!" Matthew raised his eyebrows. Well! This was interesting. He had no time to reflect on it, though, since Kuros was tugging at his sleeve.

"Squire!" Kuros said impatiently. "Why do we tarry? We must scale the castle walls."

Matthew smiled at the knight. "I'm sorry, Kuros," he said. "I'm ready now. Let's go!" He fell in behind Kuros, rolling his eyes.

Kuros paused for only a moment at the edge of the moat. Then he stripped off his tunic, wrapped all of his weapons inside of it, and held it over his head. "I don't *see* any alligators," he said. "I think it's safe." He waded in.

Matthew stood on the bank, trying to look down into the murky water. Alligators? He'd never even thought of the possibility. He looked up to see that Kuros had already reached the other side, safe and sound. Matthew shrugged, took off his shirt, and jumped in.

In a moment, he was hauling himself up on the other side. He shook off as much water as he could and surveyed the wall they'd have to climb. It rose straight up, as high as he could see. How would they ever climb it? Then he saw the bricks sticking out of the walls, in irregular patterns. They would have to work as footholds.

He turned to Kuros. "Ready?" he asked.

"Ready," said the knight.

They began to climb. It was hard work. They grasped at tiny handholds and hauled themselves up, feeling for secure spots to rest a foot. Matthew's arms were aching within minutes. This was much harder than anything he'd ever done in gym class: Harder than climbing ropes, harder than the pegboard, harder than the chinning bar. Every muscle in his body was screaming for rest. He let his weight sag for a moment when he thought his feet were securely placed.

And then he was falling. The brick he had been standing on had disappeared! His heart racing, he grabbed wildly with both hands, desperately trying to hang on to something, anything.

He stopped his fall only a yard or so above the moat. He felt like crying. It had taken so long to get to climb even a short way up the wall, and now he was almost back where he'd started. He looked up to check on Kuros's progress, and watched as the knight made the same mistake that he had.

Kuros fell, too, scrabbling at the wall for a handhold. He caught himself finally, holding on tightly to a handhold near Matthew's. "It's one of Malkil's tricks," he said, gasping. "He watches us closely, and he does not mean to make it easy for us."

Matthew's eyes widened. Malkil was truly the most powerful wizard ever. He had control over every brick in his castle!

They began to climb again, taking care to avoid putting full weight on any one brick. Still, they fell often and it seemed to Matthew that they lost two feet of height for every one they climbed.

Matthew was exhausted. He felt like he could fall asleep right then and there, clinging on to the wall. And then he heard Kuros whooping.

"Squire!" he yelled. "Gems! Gems for the taking!" The knight held out a handful of sparkling jewels that he'd pulled from a niche in the wall.

"All right!" called Matthew. This might make climbing more fun. He felt a surge of energy, and pulled himself up to the next handhold, keeping his eyes open for the gleam of rubies.

The climbing seemed to go faster now, as Matthew and Kuros hunted for and found gems along the way. Now and then Kuros sipped from the flask that held the Potion of Levitation, which seemed to help him rise more quickly. Matthew still refused to drink the potion, and continued to struggle upward under his own power.

After what seemed like hours, Matthew looked up to check his progress. He saw the wall rising above him still, but then it stopped as it formed a battlement. He looked around for Kuros, to point out how close they finally were. But Kuros was nowhere to be seen.

Matthew froze. He'd been concentrating so much on his own climbing and on his search for gems that he'd lost track of Kuros. Had the knight fallen all the way down into the moat? "Kuros!" he cried in a wavering voice. He cleared his throat. "Kuros!" he called, louder this time. "Where are you?"

"Up here, Squire!" called the knight. "And you should see the view!" Matthew looked up and saw Kuros standing on top of the battlement. "Hurry, Squire!" called Kuros.

Matthew climbed even harder, now that the end was in sight. He felt like this wall had gone on forever, and he couldn't wait to stand on solid ground again. His arms were about to give out when he finally hauled himself up onto the edge of the battlement wall. Kuros grabbed his sleeve and helped him over.

"We did it, Squire!" Kuros was exultant. He held up his hand and Matthew slapped it tiredly.

"Now what?" asked Matthew. "Where's the door into the castle?" The clouds in the sky around them were turning purple. The sun was almost down.

"Well, that's the only problem," admitted

Kuros sheepishly. "There should be a door here, but there isn't one. Methinks Malkil has made it disappear."

Matthew looked at Kuros with disbelief. "You're kidding, right? You must be kidding. We can't have climbed all this way for nothing." Matthew could see no way out of the mess they were in now. He was too depressed to protest when Kuros grabbed his arm and led him to the edge of the battlement.

"Look down, Squire," the knight said. "Do you see that dark spot?" They were looking down at the other side of the tower they'd just climbed. "Methinks it is the secret entrance I've heard legend of."

"So what?" said Matthew tiredly. "We have no way of getting to it. Climbing up was hard enough. Climbing down would be impossible."

Instead of answering, Kuros put his arm around Matthew's waist, lifted him to the edge of the battlement wall, and holding him tightly, leapt off.

Chapter Eighteen

"What are you doing?" Matthew screamed, as they fell together, plummeting toward the moat far, far below. The air rushed by his face, blowing back his hair.

"The feather, Squire!" yelled Kuros. "In your pocket. Do you not still carry it?" They fell faster every moment. "Pull it out, Squire!"

Matthew came to his senses. The feather. Of course. He fumbled in his pocket and found it. He pulled it out and held it in front of him, into the rushing wind.

Their headlong fall slowed to a gradual drift, and Matthew's heart slowed down soon after. He looked into Kuros's eyes. "I can't believe you did that," he said. "And I can't believe we're safe."

"Safe for now, Squire," answered Kuros. "But now we enter the castle and we may not be safe again for a long, long time." The knight looked grim.

They had landed softly just on the threshold of the secret entrance. Matthew took a deep breath as Kuros pushed on the door.

The door didn't budge. "Confound it!" said Kuros. "It's locked." He dug into his pocket and pulled out a key. "Perhaps this will work," he said.

It didn't.

Matthew pulled out all the keys in his pocket. He had blue keys and red keys and pink keys — all the keys he'd found and saved during their long journey. One by one they tried them all. None of them opened the door.

"Now what?" he said. This was too much. He didn't even really want to get into the castle anyway, if it was going to be as dangerous as Kuros suggested. Matthew wished he could just click his heels and be home, like Dorothy in *The Wizard of Oz*. Kuros looked just as dispirited as Matthew felt.

Then the knight's eyes lit up. "Wait, Squire!" he said. "Do not despair." He reached down into his right boot and felt around. Then he straightened up. He held up a key. "This is the last one," he said. If this does not work, our quest is failed."

Matthew held his breath as Kuros tried the key in the lock. He didn't even know what he was hoping for — that it would work? That it wouldn't?

It worked. The door swung open with a loud creaking sound. Matthew peered inside and saw an endless dark tunnel. He looked back at Kuros and shrugged. They entered, and the door swung shut behind them with a solid slam. There was no going back.

Now they were standing in pitch-black darkness. Matthew felt along the wall, and took a step forward. Kuros was at his side. How would they ever find their way?

And then, suddenly, it wasn't dark anymore. A long line of torches, blazing bundles of sticks, lit up as if on cue. They lit the tunnel until it was as bright as day. Matthew and Kuros exchanged a look. Malkil knew they were coming.

They began to walk, and before they'd gone five steps, the attacks began. First it was a band of screaming skulls. And as soon as Kuros had destroyed the last one, the bats swooped in. Matthew flattened himself against the wall of the tunnel, but as usual the creatures ignored him. He watched Kuros fight off his enemies, and noticed that the knight barely worked up a sweat. He was clearly conserving his energy.

They walked on. Without any warning, a huge goblet full of boiling liquid appeared in the air over Kuros's head. Matthew shoved him out of the way just in time. The goblet tipped and its contents streamed to the floor, sizzling through two feet of solid stone. Kuros wiped his brow.

They followed the twists and turns of the tunnel, working on instinct to find their way through the maze of passages. Occasionally, locked doors would block their path, but the keys they carried opened each door.

Matthew sniffed. The air was beginning to smell stale, and kind of like rotten eggs. He could feel that they were getting closer to Malkil. He and Kuros had stopped talking much. They were concentrating on finding their way through the castle.

Kuros broke the silence. "Winged Goblins!" he shouted. "Watch out!"

Matthew ducked as the horrible creatures flew toward him. They were incredibly ugly, and meaner-looking than anything he'd yet seen. But they didn't seem to see him. They dove straight at Kuros. The knight pulled up his Shield of Protection and drew the Wand of Wonder from its sheath at his side. The goblins froze in midflight.

Kuros dodged their hovering bodies and hurried to Matthew's side. "Quickly, Squire," he said. "Before they come back to life."

They ran down the corridor until they came to another door. When they had unlocked it, they found themselves in a different kind of tunnel. This one was more like a hall in a grand house. Chandeliers hung from the ceiling, and paintings lined the walls. Beautiful tapestry rugs lay on the floor.

Matthew looked around in wonder. What an incredible place this was! He began to walk, looking at the portraits as he passed. The eyes of the people in the paintings seemed to follow his every move. He shivered.

Kuros had wandered ahead. Suddenly, Matthew heard a deafening crash as a chandelier fell to the floor, narrowly missing the knight. This place was full of booby traps.

Matthew caught up with Kuros and they walked cautiously on. The hall was completely silent except for the sputtering of the burning torches that continued to light their way. They turned a corner in the hall, walked onto one of the gorgeous rugs that covered the floor, and fell.

The rug hadn't been covering the floor at all — it had been covering a deep, deep pit. Matthew was beyond being surprised at this point. He relaxed and let himself fall.

They landed in a huge dungeonlike room. The smell of rotten eggs was stronger than ever, and Matthew could almost taste the evil that pervaded the place. At one end of the room was a huge door, strapped in black iron and guarded by a fearsome skeleton. Matthew's breath came shorter. Malkil was behind that door. There was no question about it.

Kuros stopped for a moment and seemed to draw deep inside himself for strength. He looked at Matthew, and Matthew looked steadily back. They ran through the secret handshake, just for luck.

"That guard is the Skeleton Changeling," he said. "A worthy adversary. If I do not destroy him —"

Matthew stopped him. "You will, Kuros! I know it. Go for it!"

Kuros checked BrightSword one last time and then turned to face the Skeleton Changeling. As he approached, the skeleton seemed to glow with an evil light. Kuros drew BrightSword and ran at the creature.

The skeleton jumped aside easily. Matthew watched in horror as it then grew in size until it was almost twice as big as it had been. Then it threw a bone at Kuros's head, missing him narrowly. Kuros regained his footing and thrust again with BrightSword.

Again, the skeleton jumped, grew larger and threw a bone — an even bigger bone this time. Kuros ducked and stepped back. It took him longer this time to steady himself.

Matthew watched nervously. This Skeleton Changeling was a tough fighter. And Kuros was tired. He'd been fighting for so long now, and he'd destroyed every enemy he'd encountered. How long could he keep it up?

Before Kuros could even thrust again, the skeleton attacked once more. Kuros was driven back by a hail of bones. He raised his hand as if to ward them off.

Matthew held his breath. Kuros had to

keep fighting! If he gave up now, the quest would be a failure. The skeleton renewed his attack, and Kuros fell to the ground. And then he was still.

Matthew winced and looked away. Was it all over? He looked again. Kuros was not moving at all. The skeleton moved in for the final blow.

"Help me!" a soft voice cried. "Save me, please!" Matthew turned to see who had spoken. It had to be Guinevere, the last damsel, the one that Kuros had spoken of. Sure enough, there she was, dressed in a silver gown. She was trapped in a cage of bones, off in a darkened corner of the cave.

Matthew felt helpless. Kuros was gone, and there was no way he could save the girl himself. But when he turned back to look at Kuros, the knight was no longer lying where he had been. In fact, he was nowhere to be seen.

Then Matthew saw the skeleton flinch and duck from an unseen blow. Kuros! He'd regained his strength and remembered the Cloak of Darkness! The skeleton threw bones wildly, but they dropped into the corners of the cave without hitting anything. The invisible Kuros continued to hammer away at his enemy.

From the power of the blows, Matthew knew that Kuros was using the Ax of Agor. It was clear that no other weapon would have been enough against the skeleton.

"Save me," Guinevere cried again.

Kuros poured on one last blast of blows, and finished off the skeleton. The creature exploded in a huge cloud of dust and bone. Kuros fell exhausted to the floor, the cloak slipping off his shoulders so that Matthew could see him clearly again. It was over.

Matthew helped him to his feet and they set about releasing Guinevere from her prison. She was shaken from her ordeal, and grateful for her freedom. But she begged them not to go on.

"Beyond that door waits Malkil," she said. He is invincible! I cannot bear to see such a brave knight as Kuros die." She said good-bye, weeping, and her dress turned to white as she disappeared.

But Kuros ignored her pleas. There was no stopping him now.

GAME HINT

You can beat the Demon Skull by using the Wand of Wonder to freeze his shots.

110

Chapter Nineteen

Kuros didn't even bother to try any keys in the huge locked door. Matthew watched in amazement as the knight swung the Ax of Agor once, twice, three times until the door shattered under its blows.

Then he flung the ax aside, and next to it he piled the cloak and the wand and the dagger and the shield and the flask holding the Potion of Levitation. "These weapons will do me no good now," he said to a bewildered Matthew. "Their strength is nothing against the evil magic of Malkil. I will face the wizard with my first and truest weapon, my BrightSword."

He patted the sword where it hung by his side. Then he turned and walked through the battered door. Matthew hung back for a moment, and then followed Kuros.

Now they were in the very heart of the castle. This was the wizard's domain. The hair stood up on the back of Matthew's neck. He felt evil looming, pervading the very atmosphere. His palms were wet with sweat, and he was breathing shallowly, as if to avoid the scent of evil.

He realized that here, in the presence of Malkil, he was no longer safe. He'd never been directly attacked yet in Elrond, and he was growing used to feeling invisible. He had to be careful He looked around the dank, cavernous room. Where was the wizard? Kuros was gazing steadily ahead as they walked into the center of the room. The knight looked determined and alert. Matthew gave him the 'thumbs up' sign, forgetting that Kuros would have no idea what it meant.

But Kuros gave him a tight smile. And then, there was a loud blast and a cloud of black smoke. When the smoke cleared, the wizard stood before them.

Dressed in a black cape, decorated with stars and crescent moons, the wizard grinned at them with a twisted smile. He was short, and a mop of white hair covered his tiny head.

Matthew turned white and his legs seemed to collapse. Kuros rushed to catch him, and while the knight was off guard, the wizard attacked.

A fireball flew through the air, narrowly missing Kuros's head and slamming into the wall behind him. Another followed. The wizard cackled.

Kuros helped Matthew to his feet, and shoved him toward a dark corner. But Matthew was so frightened he could barely move. He looked at the wizard. The wizard looked right back at him.

Matthew suddenly realized that the wizard was actually seeing him, as no other enemy had. And before he could duck, the wizard let a fireball fly right at him.

Matthew jumped aside, but the fireball singed his sleeve. The wizard threw another, and this one flew by his cheek. He felt its heat on his face. Matthew's mind was reeling. He was supposed to be safe in Elrond! Nothing was supposed to happen to him. But it was clear that the wizard could and would kill him, given the chance.

Matthew's legs turned to jelly again, but somehow he made them move. He had no weapons, and no skill in fighting. He would surely be killed if he did not get out of the wizard's way. He turned and took off for the nearest dark corner. Kuros took his place.

Matthew made himself as small as possible and sat watching the fight. Kuros stood his ground, thrusting and parrying bravely, ducking fireball after fireball. The wizard seemed able to appear and disappear at will, which made it next to impossible for the knight to strike a good blow.

Matthew tried to yell encouragement, but no sound emerged from his throat. He realized that the wizard must have put a spell on him. He watched Kuros fight, more frustrated than ever with his inability to help. Then he saw Kuros stumble and fall.

Malkil's back was to Matthew as he stood looming over the knight. The wizard raised his hands as he got ready to send a final, deadly fireball at Kuros. Matthew had to look away.

He turned his head, and suddenly his eyes lit up.

There, next to him on the ground, was a huge boulder. Big enough to knock down a wizard. Matthew crawled quickly over to it and threw himself against it. It didn't budge.

Matthew looked back at Kuros, who seemed frozen in place. Matthew summoned every ounce of strength he had and gave the boulder a hard shove. And it started to roll, picking up speed as it bounced toward Malkil.

Matthew saw Kuros lift his head in time to see the boulder smash into Malkil, knocking him sideways. What would have been the death-dealing fireball was deflected harmlessly into the wall as Matthew and Kuros watched.

Kuros flashed a grateful — and proud — look at Matthew. Then he jumped to his feet and attacked Malkil with renewed vigor.

Matthew watched the battle breathlessly. A moment ago it had almost ended. Kuros would have been killed, but he, Matthew, had saved him. It felt great to know he'd really made a difference. If Elrond was saved, he'd have something to do with it. But the fight wasn't over yet.

Kuros and Malkil struggled on in desperate battle. Matthew couldn't tear his eyes away. Then he heard a muffled sound nearby.

He peered into the darkness next to him. There she was. The Princess Miranda. This beautiful girl could be no one else. She was dressed in black, and bound and gagged.

He crawled over to her and helped her loosen her ties. She looked at him gratefully, but did not speak. He reached over to hold her hand, and they watched the battle together, fear in their eyes.

The sights and sounds were horrific. Matthew winced as the fireballs thrown by the wizard sizzled and shrieked through the air. BrightSword flashed and darted, drawing occasional drops of black blood from the wizard's arm and shoulder.

Kuros was tiring. Matthew could see it clearly. The wizard knew it, too. He threw a barrage of fireballs, and then disappeared for a moment. He reappeared on the other side of Kuros, and bombarded him again. The knight fell to his knees.

Then the wizard appeared directly in front of Kuros, within striking range. Summoning his last ounce of energy, Kuros rose and wielded BrightSword, sinking the blade into the wizard right up to the hilt. Then he collapsed.

A wild cackling sound filled the room as the wizard appeared behind Kuros. The "wizard" Kuros had run through with his sword had been an illusion. The real wizard was still very much alive.

GAME HINT

In the second level, it is essential that you find the Boots of Lava Walk. Even though you have to give up the Boots of Force, you'll need the Boots of Lava Walk for Level 3.

Chapter Twenty

Matthew couldn't look. He didn't think he could stand seeing Kuros die.

He felt Princess Miranda stir beside him. He looked at her. Her face was white and her eyes were wide. She looked as if she were trying to speak. She parted her parched lips. She swallowed. Then she whispered, "Kuros."

Matthew sitting right next to her, could barely hear her. But Kuros heard. Matthew turned to look at him, and saw a surge of energy fill the knight's body. Kuros rose to his feet, a gleam in his eyes.

"Kuros," the princess said, louder this time. "Kuros, my knight. I love thee."

The words had an astounding effect on Kuros. Matthew saw him spring into action and fight as he had never fought before. He beat the wizard back, thrusting constantly with BrightSword. The wizard had no time to disappear or work any other magic.

Whup-whup-whup! Matthew loved the sound of BrightSword at work. He sat up, no longer afraid to watch. Kuros was in command.

The knight delivered blow after blow. There was a final, solid lunge, and then a blinding flash. Matthew covered his eyes, fearing he would go blind from it.

And then it was over. A small pile of black gems sat on the ground where the wizard had last stood. A column of evil-smelling black smoke rose from it.

Kuros stood victorious in the middle of the room. He met Matthew's eyes and smiled.

When Matthew turned to look at Miranda, she was standing tall, freed of her ropes. She was bathed in light, glinting off her gown, which had magically become golden. Standing behind her in a half circle were the six damsels Matthew and Kuros had rescued, all of them dressed in white. Matthew's heart leapt at the sight of Grizelda, but he held back from calling out to her. Something serious was about to happen.

Princess Miranda held out her hands to Kuros, and the knight stepped forward to take them. When their hands touched, a pure white light blazed out, blinding Matthew.

Suddenly, he felt dizzy, light-headed. The room seemed to be swirling around him.

He thought he heard a voice — Kuros's voice — calling to him: "Squire . . . we shall meet again . . . farewell and a thousand thanks." The room filled up with light, then the voice faded away.

Chapter Twenty-One

Matthew shook his head and rubbed his eyes. What was happening? Where was Kuros? Where was Princess Miranda? And where, oh, where was Grizelda?

He looked around. Was he back in the forest? He didn't see any trees or vines. Or was it one of the caves he'd landed in? Then his surroundings came into focus.

His bed. His old rag rug. His dirty socks. He was home, home at last.

He sat up and stretched. His room. It looked so ordinary, so boring, so ... wonderful! It was great to be back.

He looked over at his desk. There, on top, was his notebook for creative writing. That class was going to be a breeze, now. Ms. Underhill would be amazed at some of the stuff he would be coming up with. He had enough stories to last a whole semester!

Then the front door slammed downstairs.

"Matthew? Are you home?" Oh, man! His dad was home from work. Matthew looked wildly around the room until his glance fell on the night table near his bed. There it stood, the tiny but proud figure of a knight.

Matthew picked it up. "Kuros!" he whispered to it. "Thanks for the adventure. I'll be back!" Then he wrapped his fist around the figure and slipped down the stairs. He avoided the front hallway, where his dad stood looking over the day's mail, and headed straight for his dad's study.

If only he could put the knight back before his dad noticed it was gone—but no. Just as he reached the study door, a big hand dropped onto his shoulder.

"Dad!" he said nervously. "How's it going?" He tightened his hand around the knight, but it was too late. His dad had seen the knight.

"I just..." Matthew stammered. "I mean...I...I was..."

But his dad just looked at him and smiled. "Come on," he said, his hand still firmly on Matthew's shoulder. "Mom called me to say that she wouldn't be home until late. Let's go make ourselves some dinner, and you can fill me in on what's happening in Elrond these days."

Dear Reader,

I hope you liked reading *Wizards & Warriors*. Here is a list of some other books that I thought you might like:

A Connecticut Yankee in King Arthur's Court
by Mark Twain

The Indian in the Cupboard
by Lynne Reid Banks

Knight's Castle
by Edward Eager

The Lion, the Witch, and the Wardrobe
by C.S. Lewis

Over Sea, Under Stone
by Susan Cooper

The Sword in the Stone
by T.H. White

You can find these books at your local library or bookstore. Ask your teacher or librarian for other books you might enjoy.

Best wishes,

F.X. Nine

★ WORLDS OF ★ POWER

BOOKS

by F.X. Nine

A new series of books based on your favorite Nintendo ® games!